SYRIAN BRIDES

ANNA HALABI

Second edition

Second edition
with three new stories

5.25" x 8"

172 pages
approx. 40,000 words

Times 10/13, 14
Optima 8, 24

Unless otherwise noted, epigraphs are recalled by the author
from the common heritage of Arabian culture.

First edition (2018) ISBN 9781980557371
Second edition (2019) ISBN 9781989048153

This is a work of fiction: no persons or organizations are considered real.
Should readers have any corrections, please contact the publisher.

Cover: "Tulip garden", William Morris (1834-1896)
           Victoria & Albert Museum, London

editing and design
Danielle Aubrey
Peter Geldart

Petra Books
petrabooks.ca

Reviews of the first edition

A delightful peek into the lives of Syrian women revealing the good, the bad, the sad, the funny, the warmth of a culture unknown to most American women.— B.

Brilliant short stories…Serious themes containing elements of humour reminded me of cautionary folk tales or fables. They draw from the way of life for many Syrians, but like parables, they contain universal truths. The stories emphasized the oppression of women by brutal or callous men…painful to contemplate but contained sly humour. — C.

Don't let the humor or the cheekiness of the characters fool you. There are some serious themes explored here — A.

I thoroughly enjoyed all the stories. — S.M.

…skillfully mimicked the language of Arabian folk tales to offer a trenchant portrait of the plight of women in Syria…Concealed beneath a disingenuously simple style lies a biting critique of the lot of women in Syria. — A.W.

The charms and difficulties of everyday life in the Syrian culture and customs are woven into these relatable stories, that can appeal to both male and female readers. —H-J K.

Great character development, great settings. —J.L.

Dealing with oppression in (at times) a light hearted way…— L.R.

…this book develops characters really quickly which I liked. I also liked how 'everyday' a lot of the stories are, but at the same time, each one is special.— E.G.

…a great job at making a world foreign to readers like me understandable and relatable.— S. G.

So many emotions were torn from me. I felt like I was there.— T.B.

…fascinated by the intricacies of a culture so different —A.B.

It is a wonderful insight into a culture which, up until now, I knew nothing about…Gorgeous writing from a really talented author who draws you in to each story so easily. Every story is different, and so cleverly composed. The characters are superbly drawn, the writing beautifully crafted — G.J.

…how well the author could describe the different problems faced by women in just a few pages, while maintaining a light tone. — A.M.

Some stories are really shocking, about the violence and the brave women enduring it. Others were funny and socially critical.—A.H.

The characters are memorable as they live their lives. Some love in terrible circumstances. Others incredibly funny! — L.H.

…entertained and educated.— R.W.

Some are shocking, some are funny or have an surprising turn. —L.

Like I was strolling Aleppo, gathering the sounds and flavours. —T.S.

Very nice collection of short stories. Offers insight on lives of women in Syria.— S. Ma.

…both entertaining and informative, as well as well-crafted. — F.S.

For all the strong Syrian women,
enduring battles — at home
and at war in their homeland.

Contents

Wealth comes like a turtle,
and runs away like a gazelle.[1]

---

[1] Unless otherwise noted, epigraphs are recalled by the author from the common heritage of Arabian culture.

Nobody's Bride

Abu Issam was smoking a cigarette on the sidewalk under the awning of his bakery.

"This damn rain. It's keeping the customers away," he murmured under his breath, taking a long drag on his cigarette. He pleasurably exhaled the white smoke when a young woman walked past him and into his store.

He coughed awkwardly, flicked his unfinished cigarette into a puddle on the street and fondled his thick black moustache as he followed her inside.

"*Ahlan wa sahlan*[2], Madam! It's an honor to welcome you in our bakery. Welcome! Welcome!" he babbled.

The slender woman loosened the knot under her chin and peeled the wet, white scarf off her head to reveal a long mane of black curls. The aide in the back froze next to the burning-hot oven, the metal baking tray in his hand — lined with rows of pistachio fingers — hovering in midair. He stared at the beautiful customer, his lower jaw dangling loosely from its joint.

She rummaged through her handbag and pulled out a small mirror and a tissue. She dabbed the runny kohl from under her black-rimmed eyes.

Then she peered over her own reflection and looked around the shop. Abu Issam, finally feeling noticed, repeated his warm welcome.

"What a pleasure to see a fresh face in our bakery! Welcome to my store. I am Abu Issam, owner of this humble establishment. Please, let me know what I can do for you.

---

[2] Ahlan wa sahlan: welcome.

Your wish is my command," he declared.

"Thank you, *Muallim*[3]. That's very kind of you," she replied. "I'd like to order a hundred-and-fifty *ma'amoul*[4] with date filling, please."

"Madam, please. There is no need for the formalities. Call me Abu Issam," he insisted with a sheepish grin on his lips and a flirty sparkle in his beady, brown eyes.

"Alright then, Abu Issam," she answered politely.

"As for the hundred-and-fifty *ma'amoul*. They'll be ready by this afternoon. Do you want to pick them up or would you like them delivered some place?" he asked. His smile was replaced with an earnest expression.

"No, no, no," she said, clicking her tongue in disapproval. "I need them right away. I have guests coming over in an hour."

"I'm sorry, Madam, but we're swamped with orders. After all, we are the best bakery in all of Aleppo," he said proudly, his chest puffed like a rooster. "I'll tell you what. Why don't you take fifty with you now and we'll deliver the rest later?"

He turned to his aide in the back, who was still in a trance. "Jassem! Stop staring and get me Abu Haitham's order! *Yallah*!" he yelled. "We can make a fresh batch for him later."

The boy rushed to fetch a cardboard box and handed it to his boss, who in turn set it on the counter in front of the young woman.

"There you go, Madam," he said. "Where would you like the rest delivered?"

---

[3] Muallim: literally 'teacher', used to address master craftsmen.

[4] Ma'amoul: Syrian pastry filled with dates or nuts.

"You can drop them off at my husband's store across the street. The goldsmith over there," she replied, pointing out the window.

"The goldsmith? Uh — Abu Ghassan is your husband?" stammered Abu Issam. He scratched his black toupee, shifting his hairline back by an inch. His now extended forehead emphasized the surprised look on his face.

"Yes, exactly. Abu Ghassan," she assured him.

"Then I'll deliver the remaining hundred *ma'amoul* to him personally! He's a dear neighbor, your husband. A very decent man," he praised.

"Thank you. Sweet of you to say. But now tell me, Abu Issam. How much do I owe you for the *ma'amoul*?" she asked.

"No, nothing at all. The first order is on the house for new customers. It is a tradition in my shop; so that we can have the pleasure of welcoming you here again. *Ahlan wa sahlan*," he said and smiled at her like a teenager with a crush.

The boy at the oven snorted loudly and smirked. His boss shot him a warning glare that sent him back to the counter in the back, where he slouched over the balls of dough and started kneading briskly.

"No, I can't possibly accept your generous offer, Abu Issam," the young woman protested. "Please, let me pay for the *ma'amoul*. After all, we're neighbors, not strangers."

"By *Allah,* neighbor! You're embarrassing me," he said, blushing. "But if you insist."

"I insist," she asserted, pursing her lips impatiently.

"Fine then. A hundred and fifty *ma'amoul*. That makes one thousand two hundred Liras. Let's say one thousand, *ma'alesh*[5]."

---

[5] Ma'alesh: it's OK.

"Here you go," she said, handing him a wad of cash from her purse. "One thousand Liras."

"And here are the first fifty *ma'amoul*," he replied, pushing the cardboard box on the counter towards her. "Enjoy them, *inshallah*."

"Thank you. I'm looking forward to tasting them," she said, covering her black curls with her white scarf. She bid him farewell and waved good-bye, as she walked out of the bakery.

"*Ma'asalameh*, Madam," he called. "Come back soon and enlighten our shop with your visit!"

He stared after her with a dopey grin on his face, as she rushed across the street in the pouring rain and entered Abu Ghassan's jewelry store.

❧

"Would you please show me that necklace in the window and the bracelet over there? The one with the red rubies," she asked the goldsmith behind the counter.

"Of course, Madam," replied Abu Ghassan. He reached into the display and undressed the plastic bust.

"Here you go," he said, presenting the two pieces to his new customer with the curly black hair.

"How much are they?" she asked, weighing the jewelry in her hand.

Abu Ghassan placed them on the scales and started punching his calculator with his index finger. He mumbled some numbers under his breath and scratched his shaven chin. A few moments later, he looked up at the young woman.

"I can give you the necklace for twenty thousand. The bracelet on the other hand is heavy and the ornate design is very elaborate. It's a bit more expensive. Thirty-three thousand Liras," he said.

"Do you have something heavier than this necklace? Show me that one over there," she said and pointed at the showcase behind him.

"This one, Madam?" he asked, as he retrieved a thick necklace from behind the glass. "Are you sure? It is more for older women or Bedouins. You have a slender neck and fine features. Maybe something more delicate would be more to your taste."

She wrapped her fingers around the necklace and slowly poured it from one hand into the other.

"How much is it?" she asked.

Again, the goldsmith weighed the necklace, theatrically calculated the price and determined it was worth fifty-eight thousand Liras.

"You see, Madam," he explained. "This design here was inspired by the Afghan motifs, mixed with our Arabesque patterns. I've never left the country, believe it or not," he chuckled, "but I love to experiment with exotic..."

"Then add the two bangles from over there and that cobra ring with the diamond eyes," she interrupted, pointing to the jewelry in the glass counter. "That should bring us to a total of about a hundred-and-fifty thousand. Am I right?"

Abu Ghassan, appalled by his customer's lack of appreciation for his art work, hastily weighed every piece separately and calculated their prices.

"You have a good eye, Madam," he said, giving her a suspicious look. "All six pieces would cost a hundred and fifty-four thousand Liras. But one hundred-and-fifty thousand is fine, *ma'alesh*. As you wish."

"I'll take them then," she said and rummaged through her handbag.

"Very well. Would you like me to put them in a fancy gift box for you?" he asked.

"No, that's fine. I'll just put them in my bag," she answered.

She pulled out a stack of banknotes from her purse and handed it to Abu Ghassan.

"Here are fifty thousand. My husband will bring by the rest later this afternoon. He owns the bakery across the street," she said and reached out for the necklaces.

"Abu Issam is your husband?" he asked, blinking nervously.

He yanked the jewelry back out of her hand before she could answer.

"Forgive me, Madam," he said. "Not to sound rude, but it's a lot of money. I can't just take your word for it. Why don't I put the necklaces aside for you, and your husband can pick them up when he drops off the money."

"I understand your worries but I need the necklaces now. They're a present for my mother in Damascus. The Pullman bus leaves in an hour," she urged. "Come with me to the bakery and talk to Abu Issam yourself. It'll only take a minute."

"I'd have to lock up the store then," said Abu Ghassan. He patted down his suit and fondled with his keys, jingling in his jacket pocket. He looked out at the pouring rain and winced. His nostrils flared in disgust.

The young woman peered out the window. "He's standing in the doorsill, smoking," she said. "I'll just call out to him. You won't have to leave your shop."

She wrapped her hair in her white scarf and stepped out into the rain. The goldsmith accompanied her up to the doorsill and carefully stuck his hairless head out.

"Abu Issam! Abu Issam!" she shouted across the street.

The bakery owner with a cigarette in one hand, waved at them with the other.

"You'll bring by the hundred later this afternoon, like we discussed? You'll give them to Abu Ghassan, right?" she shouted.

He shamefully turned his head and exhaled a cloud of white smoke, coughed and deliberately cleared his throat.

"Yes, neighbor, yes," yelled back. "I gave the Madam fifty already. I'll bring you the remaining hundred later. Don't worry, *Habibi*. Just give me an hour or so."

"Alright, *Akhi*[6]. Thank you for the reassurance. I'll see you later then," called goldsmith and slipped back behind his counter.

The young woman followed him into the store, leaving Abu Issam lingering on the doorstep of his bakery, puckering his lips and slowly sucking on his cigarette.

"Then everything is in order. Here you go, Madam," said Abu Ghassan.

He handed his customer the jewelry, who hurriedly flung it in her purse.

"Have a safe trip and I hope your mother likes the handicraft. Like I was saying, these are very special pieces…"

"Thank you. *Ma'al salameh*[7]," she mumbled, snapped her purse shut and rushed out the door.

"*Al-salamu alaikum*," greeted Abu Issam, as he entered the goldsmith's store. He placed a white cardboard box on the counter.

---

[6] Akhi: term of endearment, literally 'my brother'.

[7] Ma'al salameh: goodbye, literally 'with peace'.

"*Wa alaikum al-salam*!" Abu Ghassan automatically replied. "Welcome, welcome."

"I'm angry at you, neighbor! You never told me how gorgeous your wife is," said Abu Issam teasingly, with a mischievous smile on his face. He bounced his eyebrows, making his black wig dance on his head.

"*My* wife?" he asked, surprised.

"Yes, you fox! No wonder you've been hiding her all this time. Were you afraid someone would steal her away from you? How long have you two been married?"

"Twenty-six years," he answered. His forehead wrinkled in confusion at his neighbor's line of questioning. His bushy eyebrows met above his nose.

"Really? She really doesn't look her age at all. Unless you married her as a toddler," he chuckled. "You're one lucky man, my friend. She's quite a catch."

He let out a sigh of resignation.

"Anyway, here are the hundred *ma'amoul* that she ordered this morning." He pointed to the box on the counter. "Enjoy!"

"What am I supposed to do with a hundred *ma'amoul*?" asked Abu Ghassan.

"Eat them. What else? They're for your guests. Your wife ordered them this morning and asked me to bring them by when they were ready."

"*My* wife?"

"Yes, *your* wife. What is it with you, neighbor? We talked about it just this morning. I told you that I'd drop off the hundred in an hour. Are you that forgetful?"

"You said you'd bring by the *hundred thousand Liras* that you owed me," shouted Abu Ghassan.

"*A hundred thousand Liras*? Why would I bring you a hundred-thousand Liras?" exclaimed the bakery owner.

"Because, your wife bought jewelry worth a hundred-and-fifty thousand Liras! She paid fifty up front and said you'd bring by the rest later. You confirmed it from across the street," screeched Abu Ghassan, as the truth began to dawn on him.

"*My* wife? That woman said that she was *your* wife!" answered Abu Issam. "She came in, ordered a hundred-and-fifty *ma'amoul*, paid for them and asked me to bring them by as soon as they were ready."

"*Alahu akbar! Alahu akbar*! My heart! Help me, someone, please! Ya rabb!" pled the goldsmith.

He clasped his bald head with both hands and slumped into his chair.

"What's wrong, *Akhi*? You're scaring me," said Abu Issam, rushing behind the counter to assist his neighbor.

"That thief! She robbed me! A hundred-thousand Liras in gold and stones! She robbed me!" cried Abu Ghassan, the sweat gushing down his temples and in a stream from his forehead to the tip of his nose.

"You mean, that wasn't your wife?" asked Abu Issam. "I have to admit, I was a bit surprised. She is absolutely stunning."

He paused for a moment and squinted, processing this new piece of information.

"*Alahu akbar*! She stole the jewelry from you!" he exclaimed.

A mule can go to Mecca,
but it will not come back a pilgrim.

The Groom's Miracle

Bana sat on a wooden chair under the kitchen window — lonely, braiding her hair — and waiting to hear the voice of her upstairs neighbor. She'd been married for three months now and had left the house only once since her honeymoon to visit her in-laws.

Her husband, Bassam, was afraid she might stray if he let her out. He'd leave for the office in the morning and lock the large steel front door behind him. He usually only returned late in the evening, with groceries and an empty stomach, demanding his dinner.

"*Jarti*[8]? Are you there, *Rohi*[9]?"

She looked up from her braiding fingers and peered out the window. It was her neighbor Hala's voice calling her from the window above hers.

"Yes, I'm here. How are you, gorgeous?" Bana answered. She had never laid eyes on her neighbor. She assumed that she was a woman of breath-taking beauty, because she would occasionally boast about how her husband, Haitham, treated her like a queen and bought her expensive gifts.

"I'm fine, sister. Fantastic even! I was just out shopping for a new dress. My husband is taking me to the Kazem Al-Saher concert at the Amir Palace tomorrow night," she raved and paused for a reaction. When none came, she sighed and continued her monologue.

"I'm exhausted! I went to about a hundred boutiques in *Tellal*, *Mogambo* and *Nile Street*[10]. I'm telling you, *Habibti*,

---

[8] Jarti: my neighbor.

[9] Rohi: term of endearment, literally meaning 'my soul'.

I must have tried on about a thousand dresses! And finally, I found this beautiful green velvet dress in *Azizieh*[11]. You know how the Christians always have the most exquisite taste in fashion! They have dresses imported from Turkey and Lebanon. I'm telling you, they have the latest trends there! Not like the rags you get at one of those *bastas*[12] that line the *Muhalak*[13]."

"Yes, you're right! *Azizieh* is a great shopping neighborhood and the Christians are always well-dressed and trendy," Bana chipped in.

"I should have gone there first," said Hala. "Oh, *jarti*! You should see this dress! It is perfect! It has golden embroidery on the sleeves and around the collar. It will look perfect with the new gold earrings that Haitham got me last week. I told you about them. Remember? They look like big flowers with ornate petals and a red ruby in the middle."

"Yes, yes. I remember. I'm sure you'll look dazzling in your new outfit," Bana answered, bored of her only source of entertainment.

Hala noticed the lack of enthusiasm and started apologizing. "Oh, I'm sorry, sweetie! I'm so self-centered, babbling about my shopping spree. I didn't even ask how you were doing! Where are my manners? How are you today? Did you talk to your mother? How's your family?"

"Don't worry about it! I'm happy for you! And I like listening to your stories. You're my window to the outside

---

[10] Tellal, Mogambo and Nile Street: neighborhoods in Aleppo, popular for shopping.

[11] Azizieh: a neighborhood in the center of Old Aleppo, mostly inhabited by Christians.

[12] Basta: a sort of rummage table, where the goods are spread out on a blanket on the ground.

[13] Muhalak: the highway heading south from Aleppo to Damascus, popular for picnics and travelling salesmen.

world," she sighed and gave her neighbor a brief report of her family's well-being.

"My mother is fine, thank you. Everyone is fine, *alhamdulillah*[14]. My brother, Abdallah, is studying hard for the Baccalaureate. He hopes that he will pass this time, *inshallah*[15]! My mother said that he always has a book in his hand, even at the dinner table! It's been driving her crazy!"

A nostalgic smile crept across her face, as she realized how much she missed her family. She hadn't seen them since her wedding.

"But what is the point of all that studying? Isn't he going to take over your father's factory someday? Why is he torturing himself like that?"

"My father won't let him work in the family business without a high school diploma. He always says that education is important for a young man," she explained. "Oh, *jarti*! What I would give to be a man! Just for one day! I could leave this house! I could walk tall and proud through the city streets. I could speak to whomever I please and look them in the eye — instead of cowering behind my jealous husband, not daring to utter a word in public!"

"You're exaggerating, sister! Your life is not that bad. You have a wealthy husband and a big apartment with seven rooms! Thank *Allah* for all these blessings, *jarti*! You are so much luckier that many other women! And besides, your husband is only protecting your honor. He doesn't want people to think you're a filthy prostitute, talking to men and flirting with them. It's about his reputation as your husband, as well. Bassam is a righteous man, *Habibti*! Be grateful to *Allah* that He sent you such an honorable groom!"

---

[14] Alhamdulillah: literally 'thank Allah'.
[15] Inshallah: literally 'if Allah wishes'.

Hala paused then continued in a softer voice. "No man is perfect and we all have our flaws. This is the fate *Allah* has written for you. We are all His humble servants and we have to accept His will and obey his command."

Bana looked down at her bruised right arm. She suspected that her neighbor's sympathy was aroused by her screams the night before. She ran her fingers over the four long red marks, where her husband had grabbed her.

It was just another one of his outbursts. She had served green beans in tomato sauce with rice for dinner. He had just started chewing on his first bite, when he spit it out and dropped his spoon. He turned to her, a frown wrinkling his forehead. The corners of his mouth twisted in disgust.

"There's too much salt in this stew. It makes me want to vomit! Did you do this on purpose, you stupid cow? May *Allah* give me patience to put up with you!"

He stood up and waved his open palm menacingly at her like a red-hot iron. His broad shoulders and his bulging biceps were tense with anger as he hovered over his trembling wife.

"Didn't your mother teach you how to cook? You're useless! As dumb as the chair you're sitting on!"

Bana lowered her head. Her lower lip was quivering.

"I'm sorry. I swear! I only added a pinch of salt to the beans and another in the boiling water for the rice! I'm so sorry! Forgive me!" she whispered.

She desperately reached for his hand to kiss it as a sign of respect and obedience, but he quickly jerked it free.

"Are you calling me a liar, you little piece of trash? Come! Taste it!" Bassam ordered as he grabbed her arm. He pulled her off her chair and yanked her across the table. Her mouth twitched in pain as he shoved a spoon full of hot sauce into her mouth. She felt like her tongue was on fire.

"Swallow!" he barked. He threw the spoon on the floor and held her jaw shut. "I said, swallow!"

She obeyed. The flame made its way down to her stomach, torching her on the inside — stifling her cries for mercy.

"Can you taste it? Huh? This food is so salty, it's making your eyes water!"

Bana slouched over the table, clutching her throat and gasping for air. Every breath reignited the fire inside her.

"Now, get out of my sight! Go!" he roared, as he pushed her to the floor. "I don't know what *Allah* is punishing me for, that he sent me a whore like you! May He relieve me from you soon! May *Allah* send you fever and disease! I wish a car without a license plate would run you over! May The Almighty rid me of you — sooner rather than later!"

She clumsily ran towards the bedroom for shelter, like a wounded prey, while he continued to rain insults from across the hall. Tears flooded her eyes, making it hard to see where she was going. She let out an almost inaudible squeal as she stumbled over her chair.

She slammed the door behind her and crouched in the corner behind the closet, where she cried herself to sleep on the floor.

She wanted to avoid the bed and her husband's lame attempt of reconciliation. His apology was usually his excuse to force himself onto her. He disgusted her. She felt sick just thinking of his touch.

Her mother had talked her into accepting him as a husband. "Bassam is a religious man. Pious and honorable, *binti*. He will treat you with respect like our prophet Mohammad, peace and blessings be upon him, treated his wives. Even Aisha, his third wife, bore witness that *Allah*'s prophet had never beaten any woman, any servant or anything with his hand, except when fighting in the way of

The Almighty. And besides, he's so good-looking and only thirty-five years old. He's a real catch and you're not getting any younger."

She was twenty-three and felt the growing pressure of her family to find a husband. Her desperation and her father's fear of losing the wealthy candidate had led to a short engagement period of only one month. She had barely gotten to know Bassam before the wedding. They had met twice in the presence of both their families, rendering any attempt at a meaningful conversation impossible.

"What are you cooking for your husband today, sister?" Hala's voice tore Bana out of her daydream.

"Bassam brought me nettles and chicken yesterday. He wants me to make *Mloukhieh*[16] for dinner. It's his favorite dish," she answered, relieved that the subject had been changed.

"My mother brought me a kilo of fish this morning. The little ones, where you can pull the spine out like a hair out of butter. I usually like them, but I don't know...I can't stand the smell of fish lately. It makes me nauseous. Just looking at them, with their glassy eyes and that grim frown on their face makes my stomach lurch," Hala complained.

She giggled softly. "My husband, Haitham, thinks I am pregnant. He's convinced it's just morning sickness. I pray to *Allah* that he's right. It's all he talks about lately! He desperately wants a son to carry his family name! 'Call me Abu Tarek, Father of Tarek' he says, although we don't even know if I'm pregnant yet. He's such a silly man. Adorable, I'm telling you!"

Bana raised her hands in prayer. "*Inshallah, Ikhti! Inshallah!* May *Allah* send you a beautiful son, whom you

---

[16] Mloukhieh: a dish made of cooked nettles and chicken.

can rely on when you are old and who will carry your husband's name and pass it on to his sons!"

"From your lips to *Allah's* ear! Keep praying for us, *Habibti*! Pray that He blesses us with a child! I wouldn't even mind if it's a little girl...All of His gifts are sacred. Besides, I could dress her up as a princess in colorful dresses when she's little and dance at her wedding when she grows up to be a beautiful bride."

"*Inshallah*, sister," Bana sighed.

"Would you like the fish, *jarti*? It's *haram*[17] to throw it away or let it rot in the fridge."

"Thank you, *Habibti*. It's very nice of you to offer, but I'm afraid my husband will get angry if I accept gifts from the neighbors. He's a very proud man. He'll think you gave us the fish out of pity and he'll feel offended."

"Then don't tell him! Cook them for yourself when he's at work or sitting in that café down the street, playing backgammon with his bald friends, each one more obese than the other, ranting about how miserable you..."

Hala stopped midsentence, realizing that she had blurted out too much.

"I'm sorry, dearest. I can be so insensitive sometimes. My husband always warned me that I should think twice before I open my mouth. I should seal my lips and throw away the key," she sighed.

"Never mind, *jarti*. It's alright," answered Bana. The news about her husband badmouthing her in public didn't surprise her.

Hala continued in a soft, comforting voice from upstairs. "Please, *Rohi*, take the fish. You would be doing me a favor. I'll go fetch them and send down the basket."

---

[17] Haram: forbidden in Islam.

"We have seven large watermelons. Bassam bought them from Souk El-Hal at a cheap price yesterday. Now we're stuck eating watermelons for the next two weeks. Why don't I send you one of them back up? It would be a fair trade and you would be doing me a favor, because I wouldn't feel guilty about exploiting your generosity."

There was no response. Hala was already on her way to the fridge. Bana felt slightly relieved. Her counter offer was not sincere. She couldn't possibly explain it to her husband. The last time she had eaten some bread and braided cheese in his absence, he punched her so hard, she was blind in one eye for a week. A missing watermelon would probably cost her a broken bone or two.

She leaned out the window and saw the bottom of the basket coming towards her as her neighbor lowered it carefully from her window with a rope. She reached out and pulled it towards her with one hand, while she took out the plastic bag containing seven fresh cod with the other.

"Thank you, sister. May *Allah* bless you and your husband. May He reward your generosity with the tenfold!"

"Just not with more fish, *inshallah*!" she chuckled. "*Yallah*, *Habibti*, I have to start cooking now. I'm making *kibbeh*[18] with a walnut filling for my dear Haitham. I bought some fresh minced meat from the butcher in *Syriaan*[19] on my way home today. You know the one with the chopped off middle finger and the thick moustache. He has the best meat in the whole city — pure veal with extra fat. My husband is going to lick his fingers after each ball and kiss the hands that made them!"

---

[18] Kibbeh: balls of minced meat and bulgar stuffed with more minced meat and nuts.

[19] Syriaan: a district in the center of Old Aleppo, mostly inhabited by Assyrian Christians.

"Then start your cooking and enjoy your dinner, *Ikhti*. I'll talk to you tomorrow, *inshallah*. Let me know how many kisses your hands earn this evening!" Bana called.

She got up from her stool under the window and turned back to the silence of her kitchen. She thought about her husband, his mood swings and his imperturbable faith in *Allah*, when the stacked watermelons in the corner caught her eye. A conniving smile began to spread on her lips.

She grabbed the bag of fish at her feet and set them on the kitchen table. She set a tray beside them and pulled a sharp knife and a spoon out of the drawer. She heaved a watermelon onto the tray and carefully cut a small hole in the top of the fruit. Then she removed the cap and carved out a handful of the blood-red interior with the spoon. She hid one of the fish inside and padded it with the balled-out flesh. She then gently placed the top back on the melon.

She took a step back and admired her masterpiece. The modification was barely visible. The scar blended in perfectly with the dark green stripes. She returned the melon to the stack in the corner and carried another back to the table.

Bana stowed all seven fish in the seven watermelons. When she finished, she wiped off the tray and the table, destroying all traces of her undertaking. She glanced at the clock over the kitchen door. It was already six o'clock. Her husband was due back home in less than an hour. She quickly started preparing the nettles and the chicken for his dinner.

Later that night, the couple ate their dinner in silence. Bassam seemed to be lost in his thoughts. Bana did not dare interrupt the fragile peace. As she cleared the table, he got ready for his evening prayers.

"Woman! Go and get me one of the watermelons! I've been craving that sweet, red pulp all day!" he shouted out of the bathroom. He bent over the sink, performing the obligatory washing ritual of his face, forearms and feet.

Bana fetched a tray and a knife from the kitchen and set them on the coffee table in the living room. She carefully placed one of the watermelons she had prepared earlier on the tray, with the loose cap on the bottom.

Her husband disappeared into the bedroom, where he spread out his prayer rug facing Mecca. Bana could hear him murmur the Koran verses as he fell to his knees and kissed the floor in humble obedience to *Allah*.

When he reemerged, Bana was sitting on the living room couch, nervously biting her nails.

"Stop gnawing at your nails!"

He slapped her hand away from her mouth.

"It is a sin in the eyes of *Allah*! Look at your ugly hands. They're gross! Don't you have any self-control? Move, you filthy thing! Go! Sit over there!" he shouted and pointed to a chair in the corner of the room. "I don't want you near me — especially when I'm eating. I can't enjoy the watermelon at the sight of your disgusting nails."

She hastily followed his orders. Bassam sat on the couch and pulled the coffee table towards him. He praised *Allah* under his breath and started to carve the watermelon.

When he broke off the first slice, a slippery fish fell out of its core. He froze for a few seconds, staring at the unexpected find. Then he started blinking rapidly, as if to snap himself out of a trance. He held the fish up to his nose and sniffed at it loudly. He turned it from one side to the other and examined it.

"It's a fish! What a miracle! A fish in a watermelon!" exclaimed Bana, trying hard to sound surprised.

"Get me another one! Hurry!" he shouted, without looking up.

She immediately rushed to the kitchen and came back with a second melon, with one hand carefully pressed against the loose cap on the bottom. She placed it next to the first on the tray. Bassam carved out a slice and found yet another fish that his wife had hidden earlier that afternoon. He turned to her, with a swell of pride in his chest.

"You see, Bana! You see this miracle!" he said, pointing at the fish with his knife. "*Allah* has blessed me with fresh fish! It's his way of letting me know that I'm a good Muslim, a faithful slave at his mercy. He is rewarding me for my good deeds, my patience and my generosity!"

"Yes, Bassam, of course. This miracle is a sign from *Allah*, a gift for your devoutness and piety." She tried to sound convincing and almost bowed in front of her husband.

She had long grown accustomed to Bassam's exorbitant ego and his unwavering conviction that he was as holy as the Prophet Mohammad himself. Nevertheless, she was relieved her plan had succeeded and hoped that her husband's good mood would last for the next couple of days.

"Bring me the rest of the watermelons. Let's see how many fish *Allah* has sent me," he said.

Bana fetched one melon after the other while her husband dissected them. When he had found all seven hidden fish, he turned to her with a broad smile on his face. She hadn't seen him so content since their wedding.

"Go! Put the melons and the fish in the fridge. Leave this one here." He pointed to the first melon and began to gobble up a slice.

"I'm inviting the guys over for dinner tomorrow night," he announced. "I want the fish fried with garlic and dill. And make some *tarator* sauce to go with it. Don't be stingy with the spices! I know you're a horrible cook, but, in the name of *Allah*, try to get it right this time! Call your mother if you have to!"

Bana stared at the stream of red juice running down his chin. His smile had faded almost as fast as it had appeared. She cleared the table in silence and regretted not having kept the fish for herself, like her neighbor had suggested.

"Just so you know, I counted the fish! There are exactly seven!" he shouted after her. "Don't you dare hide one for yourself! *Allah*, The Omniscient, is watching you and it is clear from his blessings today that he's on my side! Don't let your appetite turn you into a thief! The Almighty punishes sinners like you with the eternal fire of *Jihanam*!"

The next morning, after breakfast, Bana hid behind the closet, while her husband got ready for work. She waited until she heard the front door click shut and his key turn in the lock, before making her way to the kitchen.

She reluctantly opened the fridge and stared at its forbidden content. She slowly started closing the door, when she suddenly stopped. Her lips pursed in determination as she yanked the door wide open, took out the fish and threw them on the counter. She began angrily chopping at them, swinging the heavy butcher's knife over and over, spraying bits and pieces of flesh and bone all over the kitchen.

A few minutes later, she stopped and stared at the massacre, panting. She dropped the cleaver on the floor, almost missing her foot and took a deep breath. For a moment, she felt relieved and satisfied, as if a weight had been lifted off her shoulders, when it suddenly occurred to her what she had done and the grave consequences that awaited her.

She quickly grabbed a bucket from under the sink and collected all the fish scraps in it. She cleaned the kitchen, scrubbed the counters and swept the floor until they were spotless. Then she took the bucket to the squatting toilet down the hall and dumped its contents into the hole in the ground. She poured buckets full of water afterwards, to make sure the fish and its smell disappeared down the drain.

"Hey neighbor! *Rohi*, are you there?" a faint yet familiar voice asked from a distance.

It was her neighbor, Hala, calling her from her kitchen window upstairs.

Shouting out a woman's first name is a taboo in Syrian culture. Like the beauty and the voice of a woman, her name had to be protected from the eyes and ears of the public. It is a common belief among pious Muslims that seeing a woman's hair or hearing her voice could turn deprived men into rabid wolves. Like their ancestor Eve who seduced Adam to commit sin, women could lure men into having lustful, unclean thoughts.

"Yes! I'm coming, *Habibti. Yallah*, I'm coming," she shouted as she rushed back to the kitchen. "How are you, gorgeous? What's new?"

"Nothing much. I'm bored. My maid just left and I don't have to prepare dinner tonight, since we're going to the Kazem Al-Saher concert this evening," sighed Hala.

"*Jarti*? Are you still there?" she asked again after a long pause. She decided to change the subject due to her neighbor's apparent lack of interest. "Did you cook the fish yet? Did they taste good?"

"The fish? Uh...Yes, they were delicious!" Bana lied. "Thank you so much, *jarti*. May *Allah* bless you for your generosity. May He bring you health and reward you with great fortune! Thank you, *Rohi*."

"How did you prepare them? With tarator? Or as a soup?" Hala persisted.

"Uh…yes, with tarator and lots of garlic. I was worried my husband would smell it on my breath last night. But I got away with it, *alhamdulillah*[20]," she laughed nervously.

"You'll have to excuse me, now, *jarti*. I hate to cut our conversation short, but I am in a bit of a hurry today. I have to finish cleaning the house and start preparing dinner for my husband and his friends this evening," she said, trying to get out of answering more awkward questions.

Later that evening, Bana heard her husband's key turn in the lock again. She ran to the bedroom to fetch her veil and tied the white scarf in a loose knot under her chin.

"*Yallah, yallah!*" Bassam called through the door. "Are you covered, woman?"

"Yes, yes. I am covered from head to toe. Please welcome your guests into our home," she replied politely and rushed to hide in the kitchen. She closed her eyes and took a deep breath, preparing for the dreadful confrontation she was about to face.

"Come in, *Shabab*[21]!" He opened the front door and ushered two bald men, with thick, black moustaches into the dining room.

"Welcome, welcome! Make yourselves comfortable while I go fetch our dinner from the kitchen. I'm telling you, it's going to be a feast. Not only is this fish fat and fresh, but

---

[20] Alhamdulillah: thank God.

[21] Shabab: literally means 'young men', but often used to address friends.

it is blessed by *Allah* Himself. He sent me seven of them as a gift for my good morals and my generous donations to the mosque," he boasted.

Bana stood at the sink, staring at the floor and listening to his voice coming closer.

"Here you go, *Ibn Aami*[22]," she said in a trembling voice as he entered the kitchen. "I made white beans with minced meat in tomato sauce and rice. I spent all afternoon cooking. I even called my mother this morning. She guided me through the entire recipe, step-by-step. I hope you and your friends enjoy it."

"Beans? Where's the fish from last night? Did you eat it yourself, you greedy thief?!" Bassam exploded. He raised his right hand above his head, preparing to slap his wife.

"No! I mean, I don't know what you're talking about. I swear," Bana wept as she dropped to her knees, begging for mercy. "Please, believe me! I didn't eat anything for lunch. I don't know what fish you're talking about."

"Get up!" he grabbed her by the ear and heaved her to her feet. His other hand was clenched into an angry fist. "You bitch! You dare embarrass me in front of my friends! Then you have the audacity of denying it! I swear, I'll break every bone in your body with my bare hands! You filthy criminal!"

Bana felt her left cheek bone crack as her husband punched her in the face. She started screaming at the top of her lungs, when another blow to her stomach took her breath away. She gasped for air as she tried to crawl away from her attacker on all fours. He grabbed her ankles and pulled her towards him. She tried getting up, but his elbow struck her spine sending her back to the floor.

---

[22] Ibn Aami: cousin, literally son of my paternal uncle. It is a common reference of a wife to her husband, since marriages amongst relatives are customary.

"Bassam! What are you doing? Stop!" demanded a man's voice. Bana looked up and saw two burly men standing in the kitchen doorway.

"May *Allah* forgive you, brother! It is *haram* to raise your hand in anger, especially towards your wife," said the shorter of the two.

"Abu Abdo is right. Not even our Prophet Mohammad, peace and blessings be upon him, hit his wife. Have mercy, my friend, for *Allah* is merciful and compassionate. What could this frail creature have possibly done to deserve such a beating?" asked the tall one.

"Her? Frail creature? She is the reincarnation of the *Shaitan*[23] from hell. She stole the fish I found in the watermelons yesterday. Only *Allah* knows what this gluttonous hag did with seven fish!" answered Bassam. He wiped the pearls of sweat from his forehead with his sleeve. His face twitched in disgust.

"You can't be serious about the fish in the watermelon? We thought it was a joke or some kind of lame excuse to invite us over for dinner," said Abu Abdo. He gave his friend a nervous glance and the two men chuckled synchronously.

"You two clowns think I would lie about a gift from *Allah*? Why? To impress you? I don't need your approval. I am a man of spotless reputation in this city. Ask anyone in all of Aleppo. They will tell you that Bassam Kayali is an obedient servant of The Almighty and a model Muslim. I am known for my faith and my honesty. When I tell you that I found seven fish in seven watermelons, then it is nothing but the truth!"

He turned to his wife. "And if this wretched insect would stop lying, she would bear witness to that fact. She saw me

---

[23] Shaitan: Arabic for the devil. The word Satan is derived from it.

cut the melons last night. Tell them, woman! And don't you dare lie again! Speak!"

"In *Allah's* name, the Merciful, I don't know what you're talking about, Bassam. I swear, I am telling the truth," Bana cried. "I remember, how you cut all seven melons yesterday. But you said you wanted to find the sweetest one for your friends this evening. You are always so generous towards your guests and so…"

"Shut up, you, lying whore!" He interrupted her attempt to soothe him with compliments and raised his fist to give her another blow.

The two men rushed towards him. Abu Abdo stopped his hand in mid-air before it reached his wife's sore face.

"Bassam! Cut it out! Now!" he shouted.

They restrained the angry man, each locking down an arm behind his back. They dragged him out of the kitchen and tried to calm him down.

He quickly freed himself of their grip and stormed back into the kitchen. He started rummaging through the fridge, throwing out butter, eggs and everything in his way.

"I know what I found yesterday and I am going to find the damn fish as *Allah* is my witness!"

He continued his rant while he moved on to the garbage can under the sink.

"I'll find the bones if you ate my fish, you stupid witch! You can't fool me! I have *Allah* on my side."

He emptied the trash on the floor, fell to his knees and started digging through watermelon rind and plastic bags.

"I swear, I didn't eat anything. By *Allah*! By the life of my mother and my grandmother's grave! I didn't eat your fish!" sobbed Bana. She sat on the kitchen floor where he had left her, with one hand caressing her throbbing cheek.

Bassam, frustrated by the fruitless search, got up and rushed towards her. He grabbed her arm, while she screeched in pain. His friends could no longer endure the sight of the pitiful victim. They separated the married couple and forced the husband to the floor.

"Hold him down, Abu Nasser. Do you have him?" asked Abu Abdo.

"Yes, I got him," the other answered. He knelt onto Bassam's back, like he was subduing a criminal. Then he turned to the scared woman, who was curled up in the corner. "You! Go get some rope! Stop crying and get some strong rope!"

Bana, startled at being spoken to by the stranger, suddenly stopped weeping. After a moment of hesitation, she wiped her runny nose with the sleeve of her *galabieh*[24] and quickly got up. She tucked a loose strand of hair under her scarf, as if to restore her dignity and ran out of the kitchen. She returned with a thick rope from her husband's tool cupboard and handed it to the men. They quickly tied Bassam's arms behind his back.

"What are you doing? Let me go, you monkeys! Damn you both!" he cursed. "Did she tell you to tie me up like this? She's a liar and a thief!"

The men ignored his vulgar protests.

Bassam, realizing the insults weren't getting him out of his predicament, decided to try to reason with his friends.

"Let me go, *Shabab*! You know me. You know I am a religious man. I'm respected in our community. Come on...we've known each other for years."

"Yes, we've known you for years and we know what you're capable of. We're not going to have your poor wife's blood on our hands. We're taking you to the police station. Let them decide what to do with you!" said Abu Abdo.

---

[24] Galabieh: traditional Syrian house dress.

"Police? Come on…there is no need for that. Let's sit down and talk about this over a cup of tea," pled Bassam. His frown had softened as he tried to mask his fear with a nervous smile.

"I think you finally lost your mind. It wasn't Allah who sent you a miracle but the devil, who whispered in your ear. The police will take care of you. They'll send you to the *Asfurieh*[25] until you stop hallucinating," said Abu Nasser. "A fish in a watermelon…"

He shook his head and snorted incredulously. The two men shoved Bassam out the front door and into the stairwell. Bana followed them and watched her husband kicking and protesting.

"You wicked witch! Wait until I get my hands on you! I am going to kill you! You despicable piece of trash! I know you're lying! You ate the fish! I know it!" he screamed over his shoulder as the men dragged him away.

"What's going on here? What's this commotion all about? Should I call the police?" A familiar voice asked from top of the stairs.

Bana looked up to see a tall, slim woman with long, wavy, brown hair standing in front of the neighbor's front door. She was wearing large, golden earrings and a beautiful, green dress.

It was Hala — as gorgeous as she had imagined her to be. Bana could finally put a face to the soft voice that had comforted her and kept her company for the past few months.

"This man has gone crazy. He claims he found cod in a watermelon last night. And not only one, but seven in total!" explained Abu Nasser. "We're taking him to the police station before he kills his wife over this outrageous lie."

---

[25] Asfurieh: mental institution, literally means 'bird place'.

"Fish in a watermelon?" asked Hala, wrinkling her forehead in disbelief. "I've definitely never heard that one before. You'd better take him straight to the mental hospital."

She turned to Bana and noticed the nervous look on her neighbor's face. Her frown turned into a smile as she pressed the tip of her finger to her lips and gave her a wink.

None but a noble man treats women
in an honorable manner, and none
but an ignorant treats women disgracefully.

– Hadith

The Nostalgic Groom

"Hurry up, Jamila! We're going to be late!" shouted Hassan down the hallway. "It's going to be impossible to get a taxi now. It's Ramadan and the sun will set in half an hour! Everyone is rushing home to break their fast," he said and let out an audible sigh.

"Bashir and his wife, Rahaf, are going to be very annoyed if we're late again," he continued. "You know how crabby they get when they're hungry."

He examined his tie in the mirror and brushed his moustache with the comb he pulled out of his jacket pocket.

His wife finally appeared from the master bedroom. She was wearing a long sleeve, mustard-colored dress. She hurriedly made her way towards the front door, frantically slipping on her heels under her long dress.

"I'm coming! Yallah! I'm ready! Pass me my black scarf. The one with the white embroidery," she said, stretching her arm out towards the coat rack.

"Uff! Is there any color in your makeup set that you didn't smear on your face? You look like you plunged your head in a rainbow," he exclaimed and threw the veil at her.

"You are so charming, as usual," she grunted and covered her hair.

"I'm sorry, Habibti. That was rude of me. You know how I tend to lash out when I'm hungry," he apologized.

He opened the door and ushered her out.

"You know, Habibti, my first wife, Munira, Allah bless her soul. She barely wore any makeup. Just a bit of mascara on special occasions and a touch of subtle pink lipstick," he said as he locked the door behind him.

"Yes, you might have mentioned that once or twice. May she rest in peace. I'm sure she was a wonderful woman," replied Jamila, rolling her eyes.

"She had this natural beauty. Like a glow," he continued. "And she was so elegant. She always had the right dress for every occasion. She didn't have to try on seven different outfits and eight pairs of shoes."

"Yes, I know, I know. Now let's hurry and try to find a cab," she urged. She rushed down the stairs, trying to escape her husband's nostalgia.

❧

"The meal was delicious, Rahaf. Thank you and may Allah bless these hands of yours. I wish I could come here every evening to savor your cooking," said Hassan. "Bashir is very lucky to have you. I'm surprised his belly didn't grow to the size of a watermelon since you got married last year."

The four friends chuckled politely while the blushing hostess cleared the table.

"Thank you, Hassan. That's kind of you to say and you are both always welcome to join us for dinner, whenever you like," she replied.

"Yes, it was exquisite," Jamila chipped in. "I wish I could cook like you. You'll have to give me a crash course someday."

"You know, my first wife, Munira, was an excellent cook," said Hassan. "Eating at home was better than in any restaurant. I used to lick my fingers after each bite, just to savor every bit of the meal."

Rahaf glanced at her friend Jamila, who was awkwardly covering the mortified look in her eyes with one hand and nudging her husband under the table with the other.

Oblivious of her obvious discomfort and the subtle attempt to stop his monologue, Hassan resumed praising his deceased first wife.

"Her cooking was exotic though. She used to prepare the eggplant dip with yoghurt instead of tahini and stuff the kibbeh with raisins instead of nuts. She didn't like nuts. She'd always say they tasted rotten," he said and laughed softly to himself.

Jamila seized her husband's short pause to intervene. She quickly stood up and began stacking the plates.

"Let me help you clear the table, Rahaf," she offered. "You've had enough work today, preparing this delicious feast. Why don't the men move on to the living room while we prepare the coffee."

"Munira, may Allah have mercy on her soul, used to love stuffing things," continued Hassan, seemingly stuck on memory lane. "She used to stuff everything. Vine leaves for yabrak[26], pastry for sambusak[27], and mehshi[28] with zucchinis, eggplants, peppers, tomatoes and even potatoes."

"How can you stuff a potato?" asked Rahaf.

Jamila sat back down and sighed in resignation. The evening dragged on into what seemed like a eulogy.

"I'm sorry I made you feel uncomfortable at dinner last night," said Hassan.

He had just returned from work with a bouquet of flowers in one hand and a cardboard box of sweets in the other. His wife was in the kitchen, washing the dishes.

---

[26] Yabrak: vine leaves stuffed with rice and minced meat.

[27] Sambusak: hand-pies stuffed with cheese or meat.

[28] Mehshi: vegetables stuffed with rice and minced meat.

"You embarrassed me in front of our friends," pouted Jamila. She dried her hands and forced a forgiving smile.

"I know. I shouldn't have praised Rahaf's cooking like that. I noticed the angry look on your face and I think her husband Bashir didn't like me complimenting his wife too much either," he said.

"That wasn't – argh, never mind," replied Jamila tensely. She took a deep breath and stared at the dirty pot in the sink.

"Anyway, I got you these to apologize for my behavior. I know how much you like gerberas. And the ma'amoul is from Mahrousse. They have the best sweets in the city. It's stuffed with the best dates from Saudi Arabia."

"Thank you. That wasn't necessary," she said in a softer voice, her face recovering from the frown.

She opened the box and took a big bite off a piece of the sweet pastry.

"You know, my first wife, Munira, used to love *ma'amoul*," said Hassan.

"Of course, she did. It's stuffed," Jamila retorted.

Her sarcasm seemed to have bounced off her husband.

"She used to nibble on a ball of ma'amoul, with her tiny mouth — like a little mouse," he said.

Jamila dropped the half-eaten candy back into the box. Hassan gave her a puzzled look.

"I don't want to ruin my appetite before dinner," she explained with a forced smile. "Go wash up, Habibi, while I set the table."

Later that same evening, the couple was watching an Egyptian soap opera on television, when Hassan let out a loud sigh.

"What's wrong, Rohi?" asked Jamila.

"Nothing, Habibti. I'm just not a big fan of this kind of shallow entertainment. A husband and his wife fighting over silly issues like which relative to visit or what cruel things the mother-in-law said. It's silly," he said.

"We can change the channel if you want. What would you like to watch?" she asked.

"My first wife, Munira, used to love watching documentaries. She was an educated woman, you know. She had a degree in literature from the Aleppo University. When she wasn't watching a feature about the animals in the Savannah or the untouched nature of the Amazon rainforest, she would curl up in that armchair over there and read a book," he said and pointed to the scruffy leather chair in the corner of the room.

"Really? She only watched documentaries on TV?" asked Jamila incredulously. She made a mental note to get rid of the chair the next day.

"I'm telling you, she barely even watched TV at all. Our friends would talk about some popular actor or singer and she wouldn't know who they meant. She'd think he was a famous poet or scientist. That is how little she cared about this kind of broadcast."

The next morning, Jamila called her friend for moral support.

"Rahaf, help me! Please! He's driving me crazy," Jamila pled into the phone. "He keeps going on and on about his first wife. About how beautiful she is and how well she cooks. You heard it with your own two ears the other night. I can't stand it anymore! I might just scream the next time he mentions her name. Tell me, Ikhti[29]! How am I supposed to compete with a dead woman?"

"Well, look on the bright side. In a way, it's romantic that he's upholding such a loving memory of his first wife. He'll be loyal to you, too, when you're deceased. Allah forbid and keep away the evil," her friend reassured her.

৵

It was almost five o'clock that same evening. Hassan was due back from work soon. Jamila had already set the table. She had prepared an opulent meal for them to break their fast at the sound of the mosque's call for prayers and the three cannonball shots at sunset.

Her husband walked in, just as she turned on the audio system. The high-pitched voice of Fairuz filled the room.

"Good evening, Habibti. How are you, dearest?" he asked.

"Alhamdulillah, I'm fine, Habibi," she replied. "The iftar[30] is ready. Why don't you go wash up? The sun is due to set in a few minutes."

"Thank you, Rohi. But why are you listening to Fairuz? I thought you hated her voice. I remember you described it as 'nasal' once," he asked.

"Yes, but your first wife, may Allah bless her soul, loved her songs. And such a wise woman like Munira Khanum, can't possibly have bad taste. So, I decided to give Fairuz another chance," replied Jamila, smiling innocently.

---

[29] Ikhti: literally 'my sister'. A term of endearment used colloquially to address friends about the same age.

[30] Iftar: The meal to end the daily fast during the holy month of Ramadan.

"Ah, alright then," he murmured and disappeared into the bathroom, while Jamila uncovered the lavish dishes of meat and vegetables.

"I see you made mehshi and kibbeh," Hassan noticed as he returned to the dining room.

"Yes, I stuffed the vegetables and the meat balls. By the way, the kibbeh filling is with raisins, not meat, just like the deceased Munira Khanum used to cook it," she said. She pulled out a chair for her perplexed husband and ushered him to the table.

"Come, Habibi. Have a seat. Is something wrong?" she asked.

"No, nothing. I'm surprised, that's all. I'm happy that you're trying out new recipes," he answered.

The couple sat in silence, staring at their empty plates, listening to the Lebanese singer's melodies and the sound of their stomachs churning.

"I think I hear the cannonballs," said Jamila eagerly.

"Then in the name of Allah, The Almighty, let us begin this meal. Thank you, ya rabb[31]," announced Hassan. He rubbed his hands while his wife scooped some vegetables onto his plate.

After dinner, Hassan leaned back in his seat, caressed his inflated belly and thanked Jamila for the delicious meal.

"I have a little present for you in the bedroom," she said as she cleared the table.

"A present? I'm intrigued. What did I do to deserve a present?" he asked and winked at her mischievously.

"You're a faithful husband, Habibi," she replied. She took him by the hand and led him to the back of the apartment, where she handed him a package with shiny blue

---

[31] Ya rabb: Oh, God!

wrapping paper. Hassan quickly tore it open and jumped back at the sight of the picture frame inside.

"What is this?" he demanded.

"It's a portrait of your beloved first wife, Munira. I thought we could hang it over our bed. That way we can honor her memory and pray for her soul every evening before going to bed," explained Jamila, fighting the urge to smirk at her husband's visible shock.

"Are you out of your mind?" he shouted, disgustedly. "I can't sleep with her watching me every night. Put it away! Quick!"

He quickly covered his present with its wrapping paper and shoved it back into her hands.

"Are you sure? I thought you'd like a reminder of her," Jamila persisted.

"I can remember Munira without seeing her picture every night before going to sleep and every morning when I wake up. And I don't need the voice of Fairuz in my head and the taste of raisins in my mouth either. I feel like I fell into a black hole and came out in a nightmare of the past," he said, shaking his head as if to shrug off the thought of his deceased wife.

"If that is what you really want, Habibi, then I won't mention her again," promised Jamila.

She walked over to the closet with a wide grin on her face and buried her husband's past under a pile of thick blankets.

46

The one-eyed person is a beauty
in the country of the blind.

Examining the Bride

"It's been a long time since we've last seen you, Um Hussam! How have you been? How is your family? *Inshallah*[32], they are all healthy and well," said Um Ahmad. She ushered her long-lost cousin into the living room.

Um Hussam removed the white scarf from her head, revealing her gray streaked brown hair. She peeled off her heavy black coat and slung it over one of the shabby green armchairs. She deliberately roamed the room, inspecting the tacky bouquet of pink nylon flowers gathering dust on the television set and the Koran excerpt hanging on the otherwise bare walls. Her face wrinkled like a raisin in dismay. It smelled of cooked nettles with a faint scent of mold from the old furniture.

She finally sighed in resignation and turned to the young hostess, who had made herself comfortable on the matching green couch and was glowing at her visitor, her dark eyes sparkling with joy.

Um Hussam sat on the edge of the armchair and flung her long mane back in pride. Her obvious discomfort started to fade as she started to brag.

"Everyone is in good health and doing well, *alhamdullilah*[33]. My husband's business is very successful. His shop is always full of thriftless customers, from the

---

[32] Inshallah: literally, if God wishes, a common expression among Arabs, both Muslims and Christians.

[33] Alhamdulillah: literally 'thank Allah'.

morning till late at night. I'm sure you remember. He sells underwear and undergarments in Khan al-Wazir[34]," she said.

"Of course, of course! I've been to his shop several times," assured Um Ahmad. "*Allah* bless him! He has a vast collection. Very fashionable designs and quite affordable, too. I actually bought the bra I'm wearing right now at his shop," she said, as she cupped her breasts. "It's gorgeous! Black with little embroidered flowers and lace all the way up the straps."

She tugged at her sleeve and started to undress. "Wait, I'll show you."

"No! No need!" Um Hussam intervened. She sprung up, extending an arm to stop her cousin from stripping. She then quickly shrugged off the horrified look on her face, straightened her shirt and forced a smile to make up for her crude reaction.

"I'm familiar with my husband's merchandise. I think I know which bra you mean. Don't trouble yourself. Please," she said.

She slid into the armchair and leaned back, as if to recover from the shock. She crossed one leg over the other and continued praising her husband.

"As I was saying, I am very blessed with my marriage. I'm sure you also remember how generous Abu Hussam is. He loves to share his good fortune. He regularly donates to the mosque and invites our friends to rich feasts in fancy restaurants. Of course, he is also generous with me. Look, he got me this bracelet just last week."

She pulled up her sleeve to reveal a thick, ornate bangle with an elaborate arabesque carved into the gold.

---

[34] Khan al-Wazir: a part of the Old Aleppo Souk where you can find cotton textiles.

"It's beautiful, sister! May *Allah* keep him safe and bless you both, *inshallah*!" replied Um Ahmad. "But where are my manners? Please forgive me, sister, I forgot to offer you a coffee! I don't know what got into me."

She jumped up and headed for the door, almost tripping over her own *galabieh*[35]. "How would you like it, *Habibti*[36], sweet or plain?"

"With a pinch of sugar, please, but I don't want to trouble you." said Um Hussam calmly. Her earnest expression briefly softened into a faint smile as she watched the chubby woman scurry towards the door.

"No trouble at all, sister! You are most welcome! It is an honor to have you in our modest home!"

Um Ahmad called down the hallway to her daughter. "Rania! Rania! Bring us two cups of coffee! *Allah* bless you! One medium for our guest and one without sugar for me. *Yallah*, *Binti*[37], *yallah*!"

"And your son, Hussam?" asked Um Ahmad eagerly. She sat back down across from her guest. "He must be a grown man by now!"

"Yes, he has grown to be a handsome young man, my Hussam, just like his father." She continued boasting, with her chest puffed out like a rooster. "He's twenty-four now and he has a head full of black hair and a thick mustache, like a Turkish Agha. He works with his father in the shop and he's studying medicine here, at the Aleppo University."

"*Mashallah*[38]! May *Allah* protect him for you! Is he married? How many children does he have?"

---

[35] Galabieh: a traditional Syrian house dress.

[36] Habibti: a term of endearment, literally meaning 'my dear'.

[37] Binti: my daughter.

[38] Mashallah: phrase to show appreciation of someone or something Literally means 'What Allah wants'.

"No, not yet. I haven't found a girl worthy of him yet," she sighed. "Each one I meet seems to be worse than the last. I don't know what to tell you, my dear cousin. You know what they say: marriage is a matter of luck and fate. Alas, our luck has failed us so far."

Um Hussam raised her hands in prayer in front of her. "*Inshallah*! *Allah* will send me a beautiful girl from a good family soon. One who is worthy of my son and I will finally be able to dance at his wedding. *Inshallah*!"

"*Inshallah*, sister, *inshallah*! But they can't all be that bad! You're exaggerating! There are plenty of beautiful girls from good families in Aleppo! I'm sure you're being far too picky."

"Listen, Um Ahmad, let me explain. Of course, everyone has their flaws and surely, my son Hussam is not perfect either. But try to understand my situation: a young man like him, who is about to become a doctor, deserves someone decent. Don't you agree?"

"Of course, *Ikhti*, of course. So, tell me, what was wrong with the last girl you saw? Which family was she from? What didn't you like about her? Was she cross-eyed or dumb like she fell on her head when she was a baby?" asked Um Ahmad.

She leaned towards her guest, hungry for gossip, giving her cousin a good view of the dark roots of her dyed blond hair.

"She was the daughter of a salesman, who sells silk scarfs in *Khan Al-Harir*. From the Sabbagh family. They're well-known and quite wealthy. I'm sure you heard of them. Her father is an honorable man with a good reputation. But his daughter…"

Um Hussam paused for dramatical effect. She rolled her eyes in disgust, held up a rejecting hand and clicked her tongue to emphasize her disapproval.

"She's beyond ugly! Hideous, I'm telling you! Hideous! Her hair is greasy like the feathers on a duck and on her chin…she has little dark hairs sticking out like the thin hairs on a corn ear, swaying with every breeze." She spread out her fingers and waved her hands in front of her.

"Uff…that bad?" asked Um Ahmad, raising a hand to her mouth to cover her shameful smile.

"I'm telling you, she looked more like a goat than a girl! And her teeth! By *Allah*! Her teeth were black and white like the keys on a piano and her smile…if you can even call it a smile! It stretches from one ear to the next, like the equator." She swiped her right index finger across her face.

"I've never seen anything like it! Never! When she laughs and rips her mouth open; it's like peering into a deep cave! And that roar she lets out! I don't know how to describe it. She sounds like a donkey on a fire truck! Anyway, that huge hole in her face explains her figure."

"Why? What was wrong with her figure? Was she fat?" asked the hostess. She was taken aback yet amused by her cousin's sudden eruption. It seemed like the question about the bridal search hit a nerve.

"Fat? She was round like a pregnant cow!" exclaimed Um Hussam, her voice growing louder with every outburst. "When her mother, Um Bassel, bless her heart, offered us some fruits, I watched that girl swallow an entire plum. The whole thing! Like it was a sip of water! It was like I was staring at a hippopotamus at the zoo devouring its lunch."

She looked like she was about to spit fire. Her eyes bulging with rage.

"And she's lazy like a slug! Her mother did all the work. She made the coffee, brought the fruits and offered us baklava, while her daughter sat there, like a queen on her throne and stuffed her face with everything sweet and greasy in front of her. And on top of all of that, she was dirty."

"Dirty? Did her clothes have stains on them?" asked Um Ahmad, curious for more gossip.

"Not only her clothes, cousin! She smelled like vinegar and onions! I don't think she's seen a bath in over a month. Her shirt was stained at the armpits, like she was hiding fried eggplants under there."

Um Hussam frantically tucked her right hand under her left armpit with a frown of disgust on her face.

"And her jump suit pants kept a diary of every meal she had taken since she's been wearing them. It ruined my appetite just looking at the girl. I dread the moment I set eyes on that beast! She almost turned me to stone!"

She slumped back in the armchair and let out an exhausted sigh. "So, tell me Um Ahmad, am I wrong to refuse to marry my dear son Hussam to a girl like her? We are all the sons and daughters of Adam and Eve and no one can claim to be better than the other, but I can't bear the thought of having grandchildren that look like her!"

"She couldn't have been that bad, Um Hussam, no one is that horrid. I can't imagine how a girl from such a renowned family could let herself go like that," replied Um Ahmad incredulously. "But never mind. *Inshallah*, you will have better luck with the next girl. "

"Now that you mentioned it, *Habibti*," said Um Hussam, with a twinkle in her eyes, "I have to admit that I came here with an ulterior motive. I heard from our Aunt Adawieh, that your daughter Rania hasn't been married yet. So, I thought I'd drop by, to catch up with you after all those years and see how you've been, my dearest cousin. And while I'm here, sneak a peek at the future bride and perceive her rumored beauty with my own eyes."

She shrugged innocently. Her eyebrows bounced up and down while her lips broke into a mischievous smile.

Um Ahmad grinned sheepishly, flattered by her cousin's interest in her daughter. "You are always welcome in our home, sister. It is a pleasure to have you here, with or without a motive! My daughter would be lucky to marry a young man like your son, from such a respected family."

"Ah! Speak of the sun and it will appear! There she is, my daughter, Rania."

Um Ahmad pointed at the open door behind her guest, where a young woman, carrying a tray with two cups of coffee and a glass of water, entered the room.

"Good morning, Auntie."

The shy voice from behind her startled Um Hussam. She immediately lunged out of her seat to snatch a cup of coffee and get a closer look at her potential daughter-in-law.

"Good morning, you gorgeous creature! You enlighten the world with your presence." She drooled over the slender brunette with the long, wavy hair and the large, dark eyes, lined with a thin frame of *kohl*[39].

"Why did you get up, Um Hussam? Please, have a seat. Don't trouble yourself," intervened Um Ahmad.

"No trouble at all. Come, sit next to me!" said the guest. She grabbed Rania's arm with one hand and pulled her in for a kiss on the cheek, while holding her coffee in the other.

"Come, sit next to me," she insisted. "Don't just stand there."

Um Hussam patted the empty seat of the armchair next to her.

"She looks like *Allah* carved her out of Italian marble, with her smooth skin and her beautiful curves," said Um Hussam admiringly, not able to take her eyes off the girl. She playfully ran her fingers through Rania's hair.

---

[39] Kohl: also known as Kajal, an eye cosmetic similar to eyeliner.

"What a beautiful mane of hair you have. Do you treat your hair with a special product?"

She wrapped a strand around her hand and yanked it forcefully.

"Ah!" Rania cried out softly, startled as her head jerked back. "Auntie, what did you do that for? You hurt me."

"Oh, I'm sorry, *Habibti*. My ring must have caught in your hair," she said, flashing her crooked teeth at her prey. "What beautiful hair! Like raw silk! Like a waterfall, flowing down onto your shoulders!"

Rania blushed. She hid a shy smile behind her hand and shamefully glanced at her frowning mother.

Um Hussam took a loud sip of her coffee and smacked her lips. She then reached for her handbag next to her chair and began rummaging through it.

"Here, Rania, crack this walnut for me, will you? I like eating nuts with my coffee."

She brushed off the walnut and handed it to the confused young woman.

"If you're craving some nuts, *Ikhti*, we have plenty of pistachios, juicy and green — fresh from the Kurds in Tel Afrin. We wanted to use them for the baklava," said Um Ahmad. "Go, *Binti*. Go get some from the kitchen for your Auntie."

Rania obediently jumped up from her seat.

"No, no. Don't get up. Stay seated, my dear. I have a walnut here and it's more than enough."

She turned to the future bride. "Open your mouth, *Habibti*, open your mouth," she urged and shoved the walnut into Rania's mouth.

Crack! The young woman freed the nut from its shell and handed it to her potential mother-in-law.

"Thank you, dear. You are indeed an angel! Here. Take this sugar-coated almond. But chew it, don't suck on it 'til it loses its taste. *Allah* bless you! Your mouth is so small. Like that of a kitten."

Rania shot a quizzical glance at her mother and crunched the almond. "It's ok, *binti*. It's what your Auntie Um Hussam wants."

"Listen to those strong teeth. She crushed the almond like it was a grape and it definitely wasn't soft," said Um Hussam, the half-eaten walnut swiveling in her mouth.

"Yes, my daughter's teeth are strong and healthy," said Um Ahmad proudly as she turned to her daughter.

"Rania, get up and get your Auntie another glass of water from the kitchen. She seems to be thirsty from the coffee and the nuts."

The young girl reluctantly got up and headed back towards the kitchen while Um Hussam admired her gait. "How elegantly she walks, like an Arabian princess! Dance barefoot on my grave, will you!" she called after Rania in awe.

"God forbid, Um Hussam!" Um Ahmad exclaimed. "But it looks like you're very fond of my daughter, am I right?" she said smiling at her guest.

Rania came back with the refilled glass and set it on the coffee table in front of Um Hussam.

"Here you go, Auntie," she whispered quietly.

"Of course. She's a diamond compared to that girl I was telling you about earlier. That one had a hunch-back like a bear and she wobbled like a walrus. Rania, on the other hand, is like a dove on an olive branch," said Um Hussam as she rummaged in her purse again.

"I forgot to take my medicine. The doctor prescribed a pill for my blood pressure. I hope I brought the right box with me. The name is printed on the package, but I can't read it. The writing is too small, like ant footprints."

She shoved the box into the young woman's lap.

"Rania, *binti*, can you read Latin letters? Tell me what that says, will you?" she asked.

"Of course, she can read. My daughter finished high school," said Um Ahmad defensively.

"This one says Aspirin," said Rania and handed back the box.

"Oh no. It's the wrong one," said Um Hussam indifferently. She snatched the box of pills and threw it back in her purse. "It's ok. I'll just take two when I get home. Rania, however, has the eyes of an eagle," she said hastily and flung her handbag on the coffee table, knocking over the glass of water.

"*Allah*, forgive me! I am so clumsy! I'm telling you, I'm like a raging storm. I knock over everything fragile and trip over anything, even pumpkin seeds."

She was obviously not a talented actress.

The young woman jumped up and ran towards the kitchen to fetch a towel. Just as she reached the doorway, Um Hussam started whispering her name. "Rania, Rania."

"Yes, Auntie?"

"How good your hearing is! Can I trouble you for another glass of water if you're heading towards the kitchen?"

"Of course, Auntie. No trouble at all," the girl replied, lowering her head humbly.

"So, did Rania pass all your tests, Um Hussam? Her hair is real. Her teeth are strong. Her sight and hearing impeccable. She is educated and polite. What more do you want in a daughter-in-law?" asked Um Ahmad tensely.

Um Hussam shrugged in shame. "Yes, yes. She passed. You raised her well," she retorted. "But there is just one last thing."

She held her hands up in front of her, like a wildcat about to pounce on a field mouse.

"I have to snatch a feel. You know how it is. Some women use sponges or tissues. Do I have to spell it out for you?"

Rania, who had just returned with a mop and another glass of water, stopped dead in her tracks. The color drained from her face.

"No, Um Hussam, that won't be necessary," objected Um Ahmad. "Rania, *binti*, go to your room."

"Good bye, Auntie," mumbled the frightened young woman and hurried out of the room.

Um Ahmad turned back to the mother of the groom.

"Don't worry, Um Hussam. Every part of my daughter's body is natural and original. Nothing has been fixed nor altered. She is just the way *Allah* created her," she insisted.

"If you say so…You know as well as I do that surgery is a deal-breaker. I was honestly thinking of taking her to the Hammam. You know what they say; it's only in the bath that you can tell the bald from the hairy. *Yallah*, I'll take your word for it. The girl left a good impression. She is pretty and well-behaved," said Um Hussam.

"Alright then. We're also interested. After all, we are related and there is no better marriage than that from one's own tribe. But I'll have to discuss the matter with the girl's father and see the young man again. The last time I saw him, he had pimples and a squeaky voice like a little girl," she replied, trying to loosen the earnest conversation with a lame joke and a forced wink.

Um Hussam ignored the attempted humor. "Of course. Take your time and discuss the matter with Abu Ahmad. I'm sure we'll come to an understanding and pay the Sheikh a visit to sign off on this marriage before *Ramadan*, *inshallah*!"

58

Trusting men is like trusting water
in a sieve.

The Bride's Maid

It all started one beautiful Tuesday morning. I was dozing off in bed, when I heard my husband singing a love song by Abdel-Halim Hafez. I got up and followed his voice to the bathroom. He was shaving off the white foam from the side of his face.

"What a beautiful voice, *Habibi*[40]! You should sell the shop and launch your career as a singer!" I said jokingly.

He turned to me and flashed me a sly smile. "Wouldn't you be jealous of all the women chasing after me, when I'm rich and famous?"

"Why would I be?" I retorted, feeling irritated by the thought of sharing my husband with his imaginary groupies. "You're a religious man and you would never summon *Allah's* wrath upon you by cheating on your wife."

"You're right, *Habibti*. Besides, how could I possibly lay eyes on any other woman? I'll never find anyone as beautiful and graceful as you, *Rohi*[41]!" He always managed to find the right words to soothe my fears.

"Come here! Let me take a closer look at that gorgeous face of yours."

He tugged at my nightgown and pulled me closer towards him. He tilted his head to one side and smiled at me as his hands caressed my cheeks. I could feel my knees weaken and turn into jelly. We had been married for almost five years, yet my husband still managed to give me butterflies.

"*Yallah, Habibi*, wash your face and get dressed," I said, as I released myself from his grasp. "I'll go make breakfast.

---

[40] Habibi: my dear.
[41] Rohi: term of endearment, literally meaning 'my soul'.

You don't want to be late for work, or you'll miss out on all the thriftless morning customers."

I made my way to the kitchen and started setting the table. I was preparing a small plate of *labneh*[42] when I noticed that the bottle of olive oil was almost empty. I saw an opportunity and decided to seize it.

I rushed to the pantry and waited until I heard my husband's footsteps. His plastic slippers slapped against the marble floor as he trudged down the hallway towards the kitchen. Just before he reached the doorway, I bent over the 10-liter tin tank of olive oil and pretended to try to heave it. As he walked in, I let out my best groan and placed one hand on my lower back, faking excruciating pain.

"What are you doing, Khadija?!" cried Moutaz, as he rushed towards me. "Let me carry that! I'll refill the oil for you. You have to be careful. The doctor said you shouldn't be doing any heavy lifting. *Allah* forbid something might happen to the baby!"

He helped me into a kitchen chair and gently laid a hand on my protruding belly. "Tell me, how is my son this morning? When can I cradle him in my arms?"

"Soon, my dear Moutaz, soon. Only a few more weeks," I replied. "To be honest, *Habibi*, it's becoming more and more difficult to clean this big apartment and cook your favorite dishes with this huge watermelon I'm carrying around in front of me all day. You deserve a good housewife and I feel like I'm failing you."

I pouted in an attempt to take advantage of his good mood.

"I'll pray to *Allah* for a dozen children from your womb. Girls and boys. So that they can lend you a hand and spoil

---

[42] Labneh: soft cheese made by straining yoghurt.

their lovely mother," he answered, ignoring my obvious hint at hiring a helping hand.

"I can't wait to see my son! He'll carry my name and take over the family business," he continued. "I've been waiting for him for fifteen years now! The wife I had before you ate every herb on the face of this earth, trying to get pregnant, but alas, her health failed her and she started withering like a fig tree in winter, until she…"

"*Allah* have mercy on her soul and may she rest peacefully in heaven! Why did you have to mention her now, Moutaz?" I interrupted. "And don't try to change the subject! I'm only seven months pregnant and I can barely stand for longer than a few minutes. What do you think will happen to me when I'm in my ninth month?"

"You are absolutely right, *Habibti*! Absolutely right! This house is too big for you to clean all by yourself. Especially in your current situation! I'm afraid your fatigue will overcome you one day and you'll fall and hurt yourself, and, *Allah* forbid, our unborn son. May He protect you both!"

He fondled my belly and gave me a forced smile. "Believe me, Khadija, I worry about you all the time. You remember the time I almost punched that beggar in the souk? Remember? He wouldn't stop hassling you and shoving his filthy hands in your face, begging you for some spare change."

"Of course, how could I forget that poor man!"

I laughed at the memory of him pretending to be a knight on a white horse. He had scared off the old toothless man, with a comical frown on his face and an inflated chest. I was perfectly capable of shooing off the hunchback myself, but I enjoyed being protected by my husband.

"*Allah* bless you, Moutaz! May you always watch over me and protect me from any harm," I said.

"It's my duty, my fragile flower! It's my duty towards you and before *Allah*," he insisted.

He raised his hands and slapped them over his head. "Shame on me, if I should ever neglect the mother of my son. Your wish is my command, *Habibti*, and your beautiful smile is my reward!"

He paused and combed his moustache with his fingertips.

"What if I got you a maid?" he suggested. "She could help you around the house, wash the laundry and take care of the cooking and cleaning."

My eyes lightened up. Finally!

"Really? Would you hire one for me?" I asked, acting surprised. "Or are those empty promises to appease your pregnant wife?"

"Why would I make a promise I don't plan on keeping? Of course, I'll hire a maid for you. I know you're used to having help around the house. Your parents have two maids cleaning up after them," he teased me with a mischievous grin on his face.

"I'm serious, Moutaz! Don't play your silly games with me!" I tried to look angry, but his smile was contagious.

"I'm not playing with you, *Rohi*. How could I refuse any wish these sweet cherry lips long for?" he reassured me.

"Oh, thank you, *Habibi*! Thank you!" I jumped up and wrapped my arms around his neck, pressing my big bump against his. "I'll cook you your favorite meal this evening! *Mehshi kussa*[43]! You'll lick your fingers after each bite and ask for more!" I promised.

"But for now, you should get going, Moutaz. May *Allah* send you squandering customers and honest workers!" I said, ushering him towards the door.

---

[43] Mehshi kussa: Zucchinis stuffed with rice and minced meat.

"Call me Abu Omar, my love, because that is what I plan on calling my son. Omar. Like the third Khalifa, leader of the Muslims and the nephew of our beloved prophet, Mohammad, *Allah* bless him."

"I agree. Omar is a beautiful name," I replied. "But what if it's a girl? Would you be disappointed?"

The question was uncalled for, since I was sure that we were having a boy. My aunt Adawiyeh's sister-in-law held a pendulum over my belly a couple of weeks ago and it swung from left to right in a straight line. She said that meant that it's a boy. If it had spun in circles, it would have been a definite sign for a girl.

"Disappointed? How can I be disappointed?" he asked. "A child is a gift from *Allah*, whether it's a boy or a girl! The most important thing is that it's healthy."

"That is what I love most about you, *Habibi*. Your strong faith and your love for *Allah*, his prophet and his religion. If it is His will, I'll give birth to our healthy son...but it would help if I had a maid," I said and gave him a wink.

"Don't worry. I won't forget your maid, but I really should get going now. I'll order the meat from the butcher and let him know you'll be picking it up this afternoon," he said. "Do you need anything else, my queen? Your wish is my command. Just tell me what you need and I will move mountains and swim across the seven seas to get you whatever it is that you long for."

I could feel my face blushing at his proclaimed devotion. "Nothing else, Abu Omar! I don't need anything else. Thank you! May the angels protect you and bring you back safe and sound."

As I closed the door behind my husband, I succumbed to daydreaming about the promised relief. I felt proud of my little trick to convince him of my need for a maid. Yet, little did I know that I would soon regret what I had wished for.

❧

That same evening, I was setting the dinner table when I heard my husband at the front door.

"Come in, *binti*, come in. No need to be ashamed," he said to the small, black burka that walked in behind him.

The woman lifted her veil and revealed the beautiful face of a young Asian princess. My face twisted into a frown as I stared at her in disgust.

Moutaz stood next to her, smiling proudly, like a little boy, who came home with good grades. "There you are, *Habibti*."

He turned back to his companion. "Go and greet your new mistress," he ordered.

"Who is this?" I asked, not bothering to hide my discontent.

"This is your new maid. Just like I promised," he said. The grin on his face was even wider now. "Did you forget our conversation this morning?"

"No, I didn't forget," I said, pursing my lips, trying to smother the anger raging inside me. I sunk into one of the dining room chairs, feeling sick to the stomach.

"I changed my mind. I don't need the help," I said, trying to sound dignified, yet my quivering voice betrayed me.

"But why not, my dear?" he walked over to me and laid a comforting hand on my shoulder. "What's wrong? You were so excited about having a maid this morning."

"That's right! I asked for a maid. An older woman with hairs sprouting out of her chin and wide hips like that of a bull! Not a twenty-year old beauty queen! I know how men's eyes tend to stray, and there is no such thing as bitter prey." I hissed, pointing to the young woman in the entrance. She was staring at her feet, visibly uncomfortable.

"You must have gone crazy! What are you talking about?" Moutaz cried out, insulted by my allegation. "May my eyeballs roll out of my head if my eyes ever stray. To me, you are the most beautiful creature in this world! You are the moon lighting up my darkest nights. No! You are even more beautiful than the moon!"

He gently nudged my chin up with his fingers.

"Look at me, *Habibti*," he said. "You are the queen and she is your slave. If we don't like her, we'll get rid of her. We'll send her back to wherever she came from! You just say the word and she'll be gone in the morning."

I gave in to his passionate words and allowed him to blind me with his metaphors.

"Come closer!" I barked at the young woman.

"Yes, *Khanum*[44]," she replied.

She walked towards me and stopped at the opposite end of the dining table, her eyes still glued to her feet.

"What's your name?" I asked.

"Mariam, *Khanum*," she whispered.

"Speak up! I can barely hear you," I shouted.

"My name is Mariam, *Khanum*," she said, lifting her head and looking me straight in the eye. She had a faint foreign accent and had trouble pronouncing some of the harsh Arabic consonants.

"Where are you from?" I asked.

"Philippines or Indonesia. Somewhere in that neighborhood," my husband interrupted nervously. "That's not important. She speaks Arabic and she's a Muslim. What more do you want?"

His hasty dismissal of my question made me even more suspicious.

---

[44] Khanum: Madam, a way to formally address a woman.

"I was talking to her! I want to hear Mariam's voice and get to know her better," I barked at him and continued the interrogation. "Your name is Mariam and you're Muslim? How did that happen?"

"I'm from the Philippines, *Khanum*. I was baptized as a Catholic, but the businessman, who bought me from my parent's house more than ten years ago, insisted I convert to Islam. He wanted his children raised by someone who believed in *Allah* and his prophet Mohammad, peace be upon him," she explained.

"Tell me, Mariam. Why did you leave that family?" I asked. I was curious and reckoned that she was fired for her looks.

She turned away and her rosy cheeks turned pale.

"Tell me! Speak!" I insisted. "Why did you leave them? They fired you, didn't they?"

"My master, he was religious during the day, preaching from the Koran and spreading *Allah's* message about the *halal* and the *haram*. But in the evenings, he would turn into Satan himself. He used to do unspeakable things to me, *Khanum*. He would drink and let out his anger and frustration on me. I was afraid of him, so one day, after he left the house and the children were at school, I gathered my few belongings and fled, for fear of my safety and sanity," she confessed.

I didn't buy the innocent act and kept drilling. "And how did you meet my husband?"

Moutaz opened his mouth, as if to interject, but Mariam was faster to reply. "When I left the villa and headed downtown, I started asking around the Souk, looking for work."

"The *Hajji*[45]," she pointed at my husband and gave him an admiring look. "I passed by his shop in Khan Al-Harir. He felt sorry for me and offered me a job in your home. He told me that his wife was a kind and loving woman."

She raised her hands in prayer. "I thanked *Allah*, the most merciful and compassionate. He who forgets no one! Not even the little mouse in the dry desert."

"People have warned me," she continued. "that not every *Hajji* is honest and not every Sheikh is pious. But I had a good feeling about the *Hajji*'s morals. And if I may say, your beauty is breath-taking, *Khanum*!"

I couldn't hold back the smile that crept over my face, despite the inept compliment.

"Stop the sweet talk! I'm not gullible. Tell me, do you know how to cook?"

"I used to cook and clean at the villa, *Khanum*. I'd mend the clothes and do the laundry, too," she said, her soft voice barely audible.

"I also took care of the children," she quickly added as her eyes wandered down to my round belly.

"Fine. Go, sit by the door over there," I said and pointed to a chair in the corner of the room. Then I turned to my husband, who was cowering in his chair like a scared rabbit.

"So, what do you think of her?" he asked anxiously.

"She seems polite and obedient," I answered, pretending to be indifferent of the competition he had brought into our home. His shoulders dropped in relief and a faint smile returned to his lips.

"My cousin, Amaal…you know her, right? She had an Asian maid, too. It was a couple of years ago. The girl committed suicide. Threw herself off the balcony!" I turned

---

[45] Hajji: a religious man who has completed the pilgrimage to Mecca, called the Hajj.

to Mariam and gave her a warning look. "I hope that doesn't happen to us."

"*Allah* forbid! I'm sure, that won't happen here, *Rohi*. That Amaal is a beast. She can even drive the demons and the *jinn* crazy. I'm surprised her husband didn't divorce her yet," said Moutaz, nervously. "Don't worry, *Habibti*, Mariam is obedient and religious. She would never jump off the balcony. Besides, we're on the first floor. She'd break a leg at most," he smirked.

I heaved myself up from the dining table and turned back to my new maid. "Come, Mariam! Follow me. I'll show you the kitchen and the maid's quarters."

She followed me down the hall to the small bathroom next to the kitchen.

"This is where you will be sleeping," I said. "It's not furnished like a palace, but it's the only empty room we have left."

I pointed to the furnace next to the door. "There's a heater in here, so it's warm in the winter. And you have your own sink and toilet, so you don't have to use ours."

I felt a twinge of guilt and quickly brushed past her and out the door. "I have a spare mattress and blankets in the master bedroom. You can come get them later. I'll bring you a cactus from the balcony, if you want to decorate your room. It blooms with pink flowers in the summer, so you'll have some color in there."

"Thank you, *Khanum*! Thank you for your generosity. *Allah* bless you and the *Hajji*. I am so grateful for your kindness," said Mariam humbly.

I suspected a hint of sarcasm, when she dropped the small flowered cloth containing all her belongings and fell to her knees. She grabbed my wrist, planted a wet kiss on the back of my hand and pressed it against her forehead in gratitude.

I tugged at my hand and freed it from her grip. There was something about this girl I didn't like, but I just couldn't put my finger on it. Her modesty seemed sincere, but my gut feeling warned me not to trust her.

❧

A few days later, my husband asked me about Mariam at the breakfast table.

"So, how's the new maid doing?"

"Better than I expected. She's hardworking and talented," I answered. I had grown accustomed to her and was thrilled with her meticulous cleaning.

"You should see the kitchen cupboards. She scrubbed them with lemon juice, till the brown marble sparkled white and she cleaned all the jars, wiped the shelves and swept all the rooms in the house, without waiting to be told. And she even put back everything in its original place. The house is more beautiful than it was before."

Moutaz smiled at me from across the table, while I raved about the help. "Your happiness gives you a warm glow," he said. "You're a sight for sore eyes, *Habibti*."

His expression then abruptly turned stern. "She's still a little girl in her twenties. She doesn't tire easily. But she's surely not a better housekeeper than you are. She's just much younger, that's all."

I ignored his hurtful remark and continued my praise. "I'm starting to like the girl. She's polite and doesn't talk back. It's just..." I hesitated to speak my mind.

"What is it?" my husband urged. "Tell me! Was she disrespectful? I'll go scold her right away! I'll make her regret she ever raised her voice at you! I'll kick her out immediately! Just say the word, *Rohi*! You are her boss. She is to respect you and follow your orders!"

"No, no, not at all. She never raised her voice. On the contrary, I can barely hear her most of the time," I exclaimed. "It's just…if only she wasn't so pretty…She's gorgeous! She looks like a mermaid from the tales of 1001 Arabian nights!"

I almost expected my husband to pretend he didn't notice her beauty, but I was about to be disappointed.

"But, *Habibti*, since when are stunning looks a flaw? It's a good thing she's pretty! Would you rather wake up to an adorable face, like a fresh flower or to that of a frowning goat? And besides, *Habibti*, *Allah* is beautiful and He loves beauty. That's why I love you, my gorgeous wife!"

He leaned forward and flashed his teeth at me in a sheepish smile.

"But, Moutaz, this girl's looks are breath-taking. Of course, her beauty does not compare to mine but still, her slanted eyes are like those of a deer and that tiny nose…" I let my voice trail off, afraid to finish my train of thought.

"What are you saying, Khadija? Are you jealous of her?" he mocked.

"How insecure do you think I am?" I retorted angrily.

He chuckled. "I didn't think so. I couldn't imagine you envying anyone for their beauty. Especially not an Asian maid."

"I'm just afraid she might feel harassed." I said, trying to disperse his suspicion. "I mean, the way the young men gape at her. The butcher's son, for example. Or that boy from the vegetable stand at the market…Oh! And that young man at the bakery — the one with the thin moustache and the greasy hair. He thinks he's prince charming and *Allah*'s gift to us women."

"You send her to the market to buy groceries?" he asked, seemingly surprised.

"How is she supposed to cook your dinner without vegetables and meat? Do you expect me to carry the heavy grocery bags all the way back home in my condition?" I replied, a bit too defensively.

"Calm down, *Habibti*. Calm down. I'll tell you what. Just let me know what you need and I'll get it for you from now on. Whatever you need — sugar, rice, vegetables, meat and all the spices on the market. I'd carry you on my eyelashes if you ask me to, my beautiful queen! Just let me know what your heart desires."

These were the words I needed to hear. Moutaz always seemed to have a sixth sense for my vulnerable moments. "Thank you, *Habibi*. I'll write you a list of tomorrow's groceries."

"Listen to me, Khadija," he said. "Listen carefully. I can't afford to do wrong by the girl. I can't have men looking at her and having filthy thoughts! Now that she's living under my roof, she is my responsibility. How will I explain myself when I stand before my Creator on Judgement Day? I'm afraid *Allah* will frown on me."

"Oh, Moutaz! I admire your faith, *Habibi*. Your righteousness and your strong morals. May *Allah* give you strength and patience, so you can continue doing good in this world."

I felt reassured that my pious husband would not be tempted. Not even by a nymph like Mariam.

"Amen and thank you for this delicious meal," he said. He set down his spoon and stood up to leave.

"But wait, darling. Take one more bite. Let me feed you one more bite," I said affectionately.

"I'll eat another hundred plates, if you feed them to me with your tender hands, even though I'm so full that I'm about to explode."

He leaned in and slurped the *mamounieh*[46] from my spoon.

I started to stack the dishes, when he objected.

"What are you doing, *Habibti*? Did you forget that you have a maid now? Let her clean up and join me for a tea on the balcony."

He wrapped his arm around me and led me to one of the chairs outside.

Feeling like a princess in a fairy tale, I called for the girl. "Mariam! Come here! Where are you? Come and clear the table!"

She appeared moments later, with a ragged, brown headscarf covering most of her silky, black hair. Her petite figure was wrapped in an old, blue house dress with a white flower embroidery around the collar.

"Right away, *sitti*[47]," she said obediently. "Can I get you anything else?"

Moutaz frowned at her and yelled, "Get us two cups of tea! And make it quick!"

❧

As the days passed, my concerns about Mariam's beauty and my husband's loyalty began to fade. Nonetheless, I kept a watchful eye on the both of them. I'd secretly peer out from behind the bedroom door and watch Moutaz walk past her in the living room on his way to work. He never seemed to notice her. Sometimes, I'd hear him bark orders at her across the apartment, like a general scolding his soldiers.

---

[46] Mamounieh: traditional Syrian breakfast dish from Aleppo with semolina.
[47] Sitti: mistress, madam.

One evening, about four weeks after Mariam had moved in with us, my husband mentioned her again at the dinner table.

"May I ask you for a small favor, *Habibti*? But don't feel obliged if it makes you feel uncomfortable," he said.

"You're making me nervous. What is it, Moutaz? What can I do for you?" I asked.

"It's nothing, really," he shrugged. "It's just that the girl…you know, your new maid…she's just…"

"What about her?" I said, frowning and bracing myself for the bad news.

"It's just that…her veil. She's very careless with her veil. It tends to slip off her head when she's doing the housework, exposing all her hair," he answered. He seemed uncomfortable and embarrassed.

"I'll talk to her. Don't worry. I'll tell her to be more careful," I assured him, relieved that the conversation did not take the ugly turn I had feared.

"I swear to you before *Allah*, Khadija!" he vowed, raising his index finger to the heavens. His voice grew louder with every syllable. "One time, she pulled up her *galabieh*, while she was washing the balcony and I accidentally caught a glimpse of her legs, all the way up to her knees."

He pulled up his right pant leg to demonstrate her sin, revealing his hairy calf.

"I'm telling you, this girl doesn't understand what it means to be a virtuous Muslim and to cover herself properly," he continued. "She wasn't raised that way. They probably walk around half naked in the Philippines, but I can't tolerate that in my house! *Allah* forgive them and have mercy on us all!"

"Moutaz! Calm down! I told you, I'll talk to her. Don't worry," I interrupted.

"It's just that she's making me sin before *Allah*," he said quietly. "What if He decides to punish us by keeping the customers away from my shop? Or what if He brings disease into our home? You know that The Almighty does not always wait till Judgement Day to punish the *kuffar*[48]! *Allah*! Forgive me! I'm begging you for mercy! I didn't mean to betray your rules and disrespect your religion," he exclaimed, raising his hands in prayer.

"*Allah* forbid! He is merciful and compassionate. I promise you, I'll talk to the girl and make sure she understands that she is welcome in this house but that there are boundaries! She can't let herself go like that," I assured him.

"Thank you, *Habibti*," he said. "I wouldn't feel comfortable talking to her myself. And I honestly thought you would be angry with me. I was afraid your jealously would blind you and that you wouldn't understand what I've been going through these last couple of weeks."

"You are underestimating me. I'm not a shallow twelve-year-old girl. I'm your wife and it's my duty to support you. Come what may. *Allah* forbid that you don't feel comfortable in your own home because of a careless maid."

I kept my promise to Moutaz and talked to the maid the very next day. I scolded her for being so profane and revealing her hair and legs in front of my husband. I ordered her to tighten her veil and tie it in a double knot under her chin so it wouldn't slip off anymore. She was to wear long underwear under her *galabieh*[49] when cleaning the house, to avoid uncovering her legs again.

---

[48] Kuffar: sinners and nonbelievers.
[49] Galabieh: traditional house dress.

আ

About three weeks after my talk with Mariam about being prudent and pious, I was having breakfast with my husband when, seemingly out of nowhere, he announced that he was going to marry her.

"Excuse me! Marry her? The maid?" I screeched. I couldn't believe what I was hearing. "What are you talking about? You can't be serious!"

"Please, Khadija, *Habibti*! Try to understand my situation," he pled. He reached out across the table to hold my hand. I quickly retracted it in disgust. He flinched and stared down at his plate.

"My reputation is ruined," he continued. "My business is going downhill. I've been losing customers. Trade deals have been falling through, because my business partners think I'm running a brothel in my house. I'm living with this woman, but I'm not related to her."

"But why do you have to marry her? By *Allah*, she's the maid!" I asked. I felt the hot tears running down my cheeks. I was devastated.

"Aaaakh, aaaakh! Why are you doing this to me, Abu Omar? Why? What will become of me? What am I going to do? Where am I supposed to go with our unborn son?" I sobbed and stroked my baby bump.

"For *Allah*'s sake, Khadija! Why can't you get it into your thick head?" he shouted and slammed his fist on the table, making the plates jump. I let out a startled cry. Moutaz stared at me for what felt like forever. His face was wrinkled into a frown. He took a deep, deliberate breath and relaunched the debate.

"The Sheikh suggested I marry her," he explained calmly. "He said it was the only way to restore my reputation and her honor. I feel sorry for the poor girl. My friends are calling her a prostitute. The marriage would only be on paper, *Habibti*. It is only so that I wouldn't be committing a sin when I see her hair or when she accidentally touches me. We would be legally wed before *Allah*."

"Touching? So, she's touching you now? Is that how she seduced you? Maybe your friends are right. She is a whore! That piece of trash! May *Allah* throw her into the eternal fires of *Jihanam*, *inshallah*! May He rid us of that homewrecker! May *Allah* send her fever and ulcers, that daughter of a donkey! That dirty bitch!" I cried.

I almost didn't recognize my own voice. It wasn't like me to use foul language and raise my voice like that. I had never felt more humiliated in my life.

"Is that all it takes? A pretty face and glossy hair? Is that all it takes for you to replace me with a younger model? Is it because I've become so fat? You don't think I'm attractive anymore. Is that it? I'm pregnant with your son! How could you do this to me?" I protested, slapping my cheeks over and over again in despair.

"Calm down, *Habibti*! Please, lower your voice!" he begged. "You're embarrassing me in front of the neighbors. What will they think of us when they hear your hysterical cries?"

"Hysterical? You dare call me hysterical, you *Ibn Al-Haram*[50]! I curse the day I agreed to marry you!"

I was on a roll. I couldn't stop ranting.

"My sister warned me about flirty men like you! She knew you would throw me out as soon as you found another victim! Men like you treat women like chewing gum. You spit them out as soon as they lose their taste! How could I have been so stupid to fall for your charms? The same

---

[50] Ibn Al-Haram: bastard, literally meaning 'son of sin'.

charms you used to lure that girl into taking my place in this house. How could I have been so naïve?"

"*Habibti, Rohi,* my queen! Calm down, *hayati*[51]! How could I replace you with anyone? There is no one like you in the entire world! You are more important to me than both my eyes! I can't live without you! I would even shave my moustache off if it made you happy! You are the mother of my son and you will always be my number one," he assured me. He gently stroked my bulging belly and leaned forward to press his lips against it.

"Don't worry, *Ibni.* Everything is going to be alright. Your mother and I are just having a little discussion," he said softly and then turned back to me. "Don't get angry, *Habibti,* please, think about our son. It must feel like a thunderstorm in there when you raise your voice like that."

"I'll talk to Mariam," he continued. "I'll make sure she understands that this marriage is only on paper and that it will change nothing around here. She will still be the maid and nothing more. She still has to obey you and kiss your feet! There's no reason for you to be worried. It's only for the good of my reputation and my business. Believe me, the way things are going at the moment, we will be broke in a month! I have no other choice."

"I believe you. I do," I whispered calmly. "May *Allah* protect us in these difficult times."

"So, do I have your blessing, *Habibti*?" he asked.

"You don't need my consent to marry again," I answered, pouting, with my arms crossed on top of my baby bump.

"You're right. The Sharia allows me to marry up to four women without even informing any of my other wives, but I

---

[51] Hayati: literally 'my life, a term of endearment like sweetie or honey.

wouldn't feel comfortable not asking for your permission. That's how much I respect you, *habibet albi*[52]," he said.

I reluctantly agreed to the marriage, wishing I had kicked Mariam out the day I met her.

ȣ

That same evening, Moutaz brought the Sheikh home for the wedding ceremony. His close friend, Abu Firas, and his shy errand boy were invited as witnesses.

The men sat in the living room, while Mariam and I cowered in the hallway behind the door. I peered through the keyhole and watched the men exchange pleasantries before getting down to business.

We listened to the Sheikh preach about the Prophet and his respect for women and the duties of a married couple.

After the short speech, he got up and walked towards the door, shuffling his feet under the enormous weight of his obese body. He opened it a crack and deliberately faced the room to avoid glancing at the women.

"Miss Mariam Kati – Kat – *Allah* help me, what is this name? Katiiigabak, daughter of Joonaathan Katig – never mind. Do you voluntarily agree to enter this marriage with Moutaz Jabri?"

The maid stared at her feet, trying to hide her smile. When she didn't react to the question, I nudged her sharply with my elbow.

"Answer the Sheikh, you rude monkey!"

"Yes, *Hajji*," she replied, stifling a giggle.

"Wipe that stupid grin off your face!" I hissed. "This marriage changes nothing! My husband is only doing this to save his reputation and your honor because you're a filthy

---

[52] Habibet albi: literally 'darling of my heart'.

whore, exposing your hair and ankles in front of strange men. Besides, your dowry is not worth more than an onion peel. You're still the maid and you always will be! Do you understand, you dirty animal?"

She gave me a long defying stare. Her narrow eyes disappeared under her thick eyelashes and her smooth forehead formed deep ripples.

"Did you receive your dowry in full?" asked the Sheikh.

"Yes, Hajji, I did," she said, her voice louder and more confident than before.

I could feel my face burning with anger as I stared back at Mariam. The gleam in her eyes made me sick to the stomach. I felt a throbbing pain in my palm. I looked down to see my long fingernails piercing my flesh in a clenched fist. I slowly turned my attention back to the open door and savored the relief of the self-inflicted agony.

"Who is present today, to witness this marriage contract?" inquired the Sheikh, as he walked back to his armchair.

"Ali Hammami, son of Moutaz Hammami, *Hajji*," announced Abu Firas from under his thick, black moustache.

The Sheikh scribbled his name into his large logbook. He then turned to the youngest of the four men and raised a quizzical eyebrow. My husband's assistant jerked back in his seat. He seemed startled at being addressed.

"Bilal Khayata, *Hajji*. Sorry. My name is Bilal Khayata," he muttered. He sat up straight and tugged at his shirt as if to adjust it. "My father's name is Talal Khayata, Your Honor."

His attendance was noted and the logbook was passed around for signatures. When it came back to the Sheikh, he examined the register and declared Moutaz and Mariam as legally wed before *Allah*. He slammed his book shut, set it on the small coffee table in front of him and leaned back in his chair as if to relax after a job well-done.

"Mariam! Where are you, Mariam?" shouted my husband.

She sprung up from next to me, covered her hair with the white veil on her shoulders and hurried into the living room.

"Yes, *Jozi*[53]?" she said with a cocky smile.

"Don't be smug," he barked. "Go get us coffee! *Yallah*! Make yourself useful! Hurry!"

The corners of her mouth dropped and her face twitched in shock. She rushed out of the room with her head down, brushed past me and into the kitchen. I followed her to relish her disappointment. I was finally able to breathe again. My husband's harsh words reassured me that nothing had changed.

A few weeks later, I was preparing to attend my cousin's wedding. It would be the last opportunity to enjoy a night out before giving birth. I toured the Old Souk for gifts and a new outfit, with Mariam at my heels carrying my shopping bags.

My husband had given me a wad of cash to splurge without putting up a fight.

"The curse has been broken and *Allah* sent a swarm of angels to bless my shop. We did right by Mariam and He is rewarding us generously," he had professed.

The next stop was the hair salon. I needed a fresh coat of makeup and bouncy curls to divert the attention from the dozens of pounds I had gained throughout the pregnancy. My friends are like cruel snakes. They would have torn me to pieces behind my back if they had seen my wry face and shaggy hair. Some say being pregnant makes a woman glow, but I had nine months of drowsiness and pimples to prove otherwise.

---

[53] Jozi: my husband.

"*Khanum*. Excuse me, *sitti*. Is it alright if I go home? I don't feel so good," murmured Mariam, snapping me out of my daydream.

The hairdresser had just started shampooing my hair. She sighed, closed the tap, wrung the water out of my hair and twirled it into a foamy, white snake on top of my head. I sat up in the armchair in front of the sink, with one hand securing the towel wrapped around my neck and turned to my servant, annoyed at the interruption.

"Now what's wrong?" I asked. "You look fine except for that distorted mouth of yours. Pull yourself together and don't grimace like that! It doesn't suit you."

I was about to lay my head back on the edge of the sink, when she continued pleading.

"It's just...I'm sorry, *sitti*, I feel nauseous, like my breakfast is making its way up my throat," she whined. "It must be because of the heat, *Khanum*. Please, let me go home. I don't want to trouble you with my ailments. May *Allah* bless you."

"Then go," I sighed, reluctantly giving in to her pleas. "You have the spare key to the house, don't you? But go straight home. No detours on the way. Make yourself some peppermint tea then lie down and rest. I need your help preparing for the party this evening. *Yallah*! Go!"

She bowed obediently, thanked me and quickly gathered the shopping bags as she scurried out, holding her scarf down with a hand on her head. She clumsily tripped over a handbag and knocked over a broom, but she didn't dare turn back or slow down.

I enjoyed the rest of my visit at the salon, rebuilding my self-esteem with a fresh coat of nail polish, a big hairstyle like those worn by the French aristocrats, and having my face repainted to resemble a marble statue with smoky cat eyes. I floated home on a cloud of well-being, feeling as beautiful as on my wedding day.

As I entered the house, humming a love song by Sabah Fakhri, I called for Mariam. There was no answer. It was quiet except for the faint sound of laughter from the back of the house.

I rushed towards the master bedroom, shouting the maid's name. I swung the bedroom door open, to surprise my husband. He let out a faint shriek and frantically began buttoning his shirt.

Mariam was sitting next to him on our bed, wearing my white lace nightgown. It seemed baggy on her slender body, sagging at the neckline, exposing her perky breasts. She quickly tugged at the sheets to cover her bare chest. She pursed her lips, feigning remorse, but the impudent twinkle in her eyes was defying.

My jaw dropped open. I could feel a pang in my chest, which gradually crawled up my throat and erupted in a gush of profanity. I didn't recognize my own voice. I couldn't remember ever hearing such vulgarities escaping my mouth. It was as if I had tapped into a deep well of obscenities that burst like a fountain.

"Calm down, *Habibti*. Calm down," begged Moutaz. He rushed towards me and grabbed my shoulders. "Khadija, please. Think of the baby! You might have a miscarriage if you have a nervous breakdown."

"The baby! You son of a bitch! You animal without shame! How could you do this to us?" I screamed.

"Khadija, please. Don't make a fuss. We weren't doing anything wrong. We are legally married before *Allah*, The Almighty, and as her husband I have the right to share a bed with her whenever I please."

I fell to my knees in resignation. Tears flooded my eyes and drained the black makeup onto my cheeks.

"Aaaakh, aaaakh, *Allah* is punishing me for my foolishness. How could I have been so naïve to believe that a man could resist his primal urges?" I cried. "Aaaakh, aaaakh, I curse the day that I agreed to let this girl into our home!"

The miserable person will be miserable
even if you hang a lantern on his head.

The Groom's Excuse

Rana paced back and forth across the living room, impatiently waiting for her husband to return. It was already nine o'clock in the evening. He hadn't shown up for lunch like he usually did and she was beginning to worry that something had happened to him. Or worse, that he was with another woman.

She heard her husband humming in the stairwell and rushed to the front door. She watched the door knob turn as she mentally prepared herself for the confrontation.

"*Al-salamu alaikum, Habibti*. How are you? Did you miss me? Why are you standing there like a welcoming committee at the airport? Where's the sign with my name on it?" said Muafak cheerfully and winked at his wife.

"Where were you?" asked Rana, crossing her arms across her chest and giving him her meanest frown.

"At work, of course. Why? What's wrong, *Rohi*[54]? You seem upset," he asked innocently.

"I just called the store. Your partner Abu Ameen said that you had left around two o'clock this afternoon and never came back," she said.

"Ah, yes, I went to the store this morning and then my sister, Hamida called. She needed help carrying a gas cartridge up to her apartment. So, I went and helped her. She insisted I stay for lunch," he explained. "You know how lonely and helpless she's been since that old husband of hers passed away. *Allah* have mercy on his soul. I told her not to marry a sixty-year-old man, no matter how rich he is. But alas, she was naïve and dreamt of being a princess."

---

[54] Rohi: term of endearment, literally meaning 'my soul'.

"Muafak. Look me in the eye and don't lie to me. I just spent the entire day with Hamida. She just left through that door a half hour ago," said Rana, pointing to the front door behind her husband.

"Ah, yes, wait. That was a couple of days ago. You're right. It couldn't have been today," he replied, sheepishly and scurried towards the kitchen. "So, what are we having for dinner this evening? Did the children eat already?"

"Yes, they ate and they are in bed. Since seven o'clock, like every day. Don't try to change the subject. Where were you? I demand an explanation!" said Rana, as she hurried after him.

"Where I was?" he asked, avoiding eye contact with his wife. He lifted the lid off one of the pots on the stove. "What did you cook today? It smells delicious. Is this *yabrak*[55]?"

"Yes, it is. Now answer me. Where were you?" she asked again.

"Well, I was on the way home for lunch, when I met Zaher Awad. You know him, right. They call him Abu Fadi. I hadn't seen him in years so I invited him to a falafel joint near the store," he said.

"Abu Fadi Awad? Didn't you tell me the other day that he emigrated to Dubai five years ago and made a fortune in real estate?" she asked, raising a suspicious eyebrow.

"Oh, yes, I forgot I told you that. No wonder I hadn't heard from him in years. Money ruins people's morals and makes you forget old friends. It's sad, Rana. Really sad, but true."

He reached into the pot and fished out a stuffed vine leaf. He examined it earnestly and nibbled on it.

"This is delicious! Give me your hands, *Habibti*. I want to kiss them for making this incredible dinner," he exclaimed

---

[55] Yabrak: vine leaves stuffed with rice and minced meat.

and reached out to embrace his wife. She quickly pulled away and perched her hands on her hips.

"Enough of the sweet-talk! Where did you really have lunch?" she insisted.

"To tell the truth, I didn't want you to hurt your feelings," he said, slowly chewing on the thin green finger and moaning in delight.

"It's alright. Tell me anyway. I can handle anything," demanded Rana.

"I went to the Gold Souk with Abu Fares to pick out a present for his wife. They had been happily married for so long and he wanted to get her something special for their tenth wedding anniversary," he explained and gobbled down another piece of *yabrak*.

"He got her a necklace. Quite a heavy thing, as thick as a baby's arm. Although frankly, I don't think she deserves it. She's a real piece of work that woman. Not like you, my sweet angel. I'd get you the moon from the sky if you ask me to," he said with a wide grin on his face.

"Didn't you say Abu Fares was a proud bachelor and that he'd never been married?" sighed Rana, tired of her husband's excuses.

"But where did he get Fares from then?" he asked, acting surprised.

"How should I know? Maybe his father's name is Fares! Who cares? For *Allah's* sake, just tell me, where you were!" she shouted, sounding desperate.

"Oh, I'm sorry, did I say Abu Fares? I meant Abu Nizar," he said, slapping his forehead. "Please excuse me, *Habibti*, I've got a lot on my mind today. I met Abu Nizar's son. You know, Nizar. And he invited me over to his house for lunch."

"Do you think I'm stupid? Abu Nizar's son is barely one year old. What did you have to eat? A bottle of milk and some porridge?"

Muafak roared with laughter. "Milk and porridge! Good one, Rana. Good joke! Really funny! Of course, I meant Abu Nizar, not his son."

He quickly brushed past her and hurried to the living room, where he sunk into one of the dark green armchairs. He was just about to reach for the TV remote when his wife rushed in.

"Abu Nizar was jailed last month for running over some bigwig general's son!" she shouted. "It was all over the news! The military police arrested him and sentenced him to twenty years in the Palmyra desert."

"What? Abu Nizar ran over a general's kid! He's in the Palmyra prison?" he exclaimed. "May *Allah* help him, that Abu Nizar. That is some really bad luck. The poor man! He's going to rot out there in the middle of the desert. He'll come out looking like a dried date, burned brown and starved to the bone! We should check up on his family and offer our support, don't you think? May *Allah* help them through these difficult times, *ya rabb*[56]!"

"Muafak! Don't drive me crazy! I asked you a simple question. Where were you? Now give me a straight answer and stop making up these silly stories," she scolded, waving a warning finger at him.

"Lower your voice, Rana, please. You'll wake the boys," he urged, slowly waving his hands, beckoning to his wife to calm down.

"Well, the truth is...*Habibti*..." he said quietly. "Technically, I didn't really have lunch. I just had a small bowl of *mouhalabieh*[57] at Sallora, the one in *Azzizieh* by the park."

He folded his hands in his lap and stared at them in shame.

---

[56] Ya rabb: Oh, God!

[57] Mouhalabieh: milky dessert.

"And with whom?" she asked accusingly as her hand moved back to her hip.

"With whom? With, uhm – Muneer Al-Kayali. He's a friend from the old neighborhood. A really nice guy. But I know you don't like him because he is so crude, so I didn't want to tell you. I wanted to avoid this awkward conversation."

He peered at his wife out of the corner of his eye, to check if she bought his excuse.

"What are you talking about?! Are you kidding? Is this some kind of sick joke? Muneer Al-Kayali died of a heart attack last year! You even went to his funeral!" she screamed.

He suddenly leapt out of his seat. "What? Muneer is dead?" he shouted, exaggerating his surprise. "No, Rana, I would never joke about something like that. *Allahu akbar!*"

He slowly sat back down, clenching the armrest for support and leaned back into his chair with a pitiful look on his face.

"Muneer is dead. The poor fellow. We were very close. We were like brothers back in grade school. He was my best friend in the neighborhood," he whined and rubbed his eyes drowsily.

"The foolish things we did together. You know, how boys can be," he chuckled nostalgically. "*Allah* bless you, Muneer, my friend. Let me read the *Al-Fatiha*[58] Surah on his soul."

He raised his hands to pray when Rana exploded in fury.

"Cut out the nonsense and tell me who you had lunch with!" she yelled. Her face was beginning to turn red and a bulging blue vein on her forehead started throbbing fiercely.

---

[58] Al-Fatiha: the first and most important Surah in the Koran.

"You want to know who I had lunch with?" he murmured, intimidated by his wife's outburst.

"Yes! Tell me!" she barked.

"You promise you won't get angry?" he asked cowardly and slumped further into his seat.

"I won't get angry!" she hollered. "Now tell me! Who did you have lunch with?"

"My mother," mumbled Muafak.

"Your mother! You left me here all by myself, cooking you a lavish meal so that you can go and eat at your mother's house? Did she spoon feed you? Did she spoil you and stuff you with one *kibbeh* after the other?"

"Calm down, *Habibti*, please, calm down. It's no big deal," he begged.

"No big deal? Did she pity our children? Did she complain about how thin you and your sons are because your wife is too lazy to prepare a proper meal? I'm sure she urged you to sneak them out to her house so that she can feed them properly. That horrid woman doesn't miss out on any opportunity to take control over our lives!" she wailed and ran out of the room sobbing.

Muafak rushed after his wife and wrapped his arms around her in an attempt to soothe her. She pushed him away and ran into the master bedroom, slamming the door behind her.

"It is my fate to be miserable. What a wretched life I'm living!" she wept.

He dragged his feet back into the living room. Her muffled cries gradually waning behind him.

He collapsed into his armchair, resting his head in his hands. He swore to himself never to tell his wife the truth again.

The successful marriage is not when you can
live in peace with your wife,
but when you can't live in peace without her.

– Yasir Qadhi [59]

---

[59] Scientist and author, b.1975.

Counterfeit Bride

The seat next to Um Rami was finally vacant. Um Nizar had been eying her neighbor all evening, lurking, waiting for an opportunity to approach her. She made her way past the dancing guests, who were swaying their hips to the voice of a Lebanese singer.

Out of the corner of her eye, she saw an elderly woman in a black dress leaning on her cane and slowly heading towards the empty chair. Um Nizar picked up the pace and shoved her way through the crowd. She almost knocked over a guest, who had just arrived and was greeting the bride on the dance floor.

"Watch where you are going! Are you blind or just cross-eyed?" shouted the young woman as she peeled off her long, olive green coat to reveal a light blue corset and matching hot pants.

Um Nizar stopped in her tracks and turned to face the loudmouth. She glared at her. Her eyes slid over the girl's voluptuous chest down to the orange peel dimples on her thick thighs, bulging from under the embroidered shorts.

"I wish I was blind! May Allah gouge my eyes out with a hot skewer to spare me the sight of this cow that squeezed itself into a rubber tube," she retorted. "Put your coat back on, binti[60]! Please! Do the world a favor and burn this outfit as soon as you get home. I'm begging you!"

---

[60] Binti: literally 'my daughter', used colloquially to address a younger woman.

She rolled her eyes at the dumbfounded guest, stuck her nose in the air and turned on her heels to continue her sprint to the much sought-after free seat.

When she finally reached the groom's mother, she awkwardly plopped into the empty chair next to her. The old woman in the black dress, who was now only an arm's length away, frowned and smacked her lips in discontent. She turned and strenuously shuffled over to the deserted table at the back of the ballroom. Um Nizar gave her a defying stare and turned back to her target.

"Alf mabrook[61]! The bride is gorgeous!" she shouted into Um Rami's ear, trying to appear casual. "I wish the couple a long and happy life together! May Allah bless your son with many children, especially boys to carry his name!"

"Thank you, Um Nizar, that's very nice of you to say! Thank you. May Allah send your son a bride as beautiful as a mermaid, *inshallah*," replied Um Rami, beaming at her neighbor.

"Your word in Allah's ear!" wished Um Nizar, holding her palms up in prayer. "So, tell me, Ikhti[62], this girl, Nahla, your daughter-in-law, is she from a good family? I mean, is she polite and obedient or is she chatty and cheeky?"

Um Rami gave her a quizzical glare, feeling insulted by the question. Subtlety was not one of Um Nizar's strong suits.

"I'm only asking – please excuse my manners – I'm looking for a bride for my youngest son," she explained. "He has a very specific image of an ideal bride in his mind. He wants a blonde girl with sky blue eyes like the European models on TV. She has to have skin as white as the inside of

---

[61] Alf mabrook: a thousand congratulations.

[62] Ikhti: literally 'my sister', a term of endearment used colloquially to address friends about the same age.

a coconut and red cheeks like shiny apples and thick eyelashes that put out a candle when she bats them, just like your son Rami's new wife! Mashallah[63]! But of course, the girl's morals and manners are the most important thing in a bride."

"My son asked me for the same characteristics when I was searching for his future wife. It's very fashionable nowadays, to marry a European looking girl," answered Um Rami. "And yes, Ikhti, Nahla is very well-behaved. She's courteous and quiet. She helps her mother around the house and only speaks when spoken to. I wouldn't have picked her for my son if she wasn't all that and more."

"Yes, Khanum, your son deserves only the best. Nothing less. So, tell me, does she have any younger sisters?" asked Um Nizar, leaning in with curiosity.

"You're in luck. She has a younger sister. Nadine. She's nineteen and her parents are looking to marry her to a suitable young man."

"Does Nadine look like her sister? Is she just as beautiful? She must be here somewhere...Point her out for me, would you?"

Um Nizar's voice trailed off as she looked around the wedding party, her head turning wildly from left to right like a nervous pigeon.

"All of Allah's creatures are beautiful, jarti[64]," sighed Um Rami, annoyed with her persistent neighbor. "Why don't you come over on Tuesday for a cup of coffee and some sweets. Then I can give you the family's phone number and tell you more about them. Let the girl enjoy her sister's wedding

---

[63] Mashallah: phrase to show appreciation of someone or something, literally means 'What Allah wants'.
[64] Jarti: my neighbor.

celebration tonight without the pressure of having to impress her future mother-in-law."

"Then, *inshallah*, I'll come by next week, Khanum[65]," Um Nizar agreed and got up to leave. "Now, please excuse me, I have to greet Um Hassan over there or she'll think I'm ignoring her. Peace be upon you, Ikhti, and a thousand congratulations for your son's marriage. Allah bless you both, ya rabb!"

Her voice trailed off as she disappeared into the crowd, chasing after another potential bride's mother.

"Thank you, Um Nizar. May Allah protect you, too," mumbled Um Rami, shaking her head at the discourtesy.

"Rami, Habibi, the room is beautiful!" exclaimed Nahla, as the newlywed couple entered their bridal suite. They had just arrived at the hotel in Kassab, where they had planned on spending their honeymoon.

"Of course! You deserve only the best, my queen," replied her new husband Rami. He tipped the bellboy, who had just set the suitcases on the luggage rack and turned to his bride.

"You should go out on the balcony," he said. He took her by the hand and led her outside. "The view of the mountains is breathtaking."

"Yes, Habibi, it's incredible. But it's a bit cold. Let me get my cardigan," she said and hurried back inside.

"Ah!" she cried a few moments later.

"What happened? Is everything alright, Rohi?" asked Rami as he rushed back into the room.

---

[65] Khanum: Madam, a way to formally address a woman.

"Yes, I'm fine. It's nothing, really. Don't worry. The zipper on my suitcase is stuck and I just broke off my nail trying to open it," she answered, holding up a long, white fingernail decorated with silver glitter.

"Oh! Allah, help us! I'll take you to the hospital immediately. You must be in excruciating pain," he cried, frantically rummaging through his pockets, looking for his car keys.

"No, don't worry. It's not that bad. It doesn't hurt at all. There is no need for a hospital," she assured him.

"Not that bad!" he exclaimed. "You broke off your entire nail! They torture criminals in prison like that. They tear off their nails with pliers!"

He stared at her for a moment, confused.

"How can you be so calm? Why aren't you bleeding?" he asked.

He fell to his knees beside her.

"Show me, Habibti. Show me," he said and gently took her hand to take a closer look at her injury.

"It's a fake nail, Habibi. They're all fake. They're glued onto my real nails," Nahla explained, as she snapped off one nail after the other. "Look. They're made of plastic."

"Your nails are fake?" asked Rami. "Alhamdulillah, you scared me half to death."

"I'm so sorry, Rohi. I tend to bite my nails when I'm nervous. They look like those of a six-year-old," she said, showing her husband her bloody, gnawed off fingertips.

"Are you disappointed in me now?" she asked bashfully.

The disgusted look on his face was abruptly replaced by a forced smile.

"No...Nahla, Habibti, Rohi! How could I ever be disappointed in you, my princess. They're just finger nails and besides, you have nothing to be nervous about now that you are my wife," he said calmly, tenderly stroking her arms.

Rami leaned in to give her a kiss, when he suddenly stopped and gently tilted her chin up.

"What's wrong, Habibi?" she asked.

He looked up at the crystal chandelier hanging from the suite's ceiling. "It must be the lighting in this room, but your eyes look so much darker than before. They're almost brown instead of the usual beautiful ocean blue," he said.

"Oh! Don't worry," she giggled. "I took out my contacts earlier. They were itching and my eyes were watering. I didn't want to look like I was crying on my first day as Mrs. Rami Attar."

"Contact lenses? Were you wearing lenses every time we met?" he asked, taking a step back, away from his new bride.

"Yes. Why? What's the big deal? My real eye color is brown, like chocolate. Don't you like my eyes anymore?" she pouted.

"No – I mean, yes, of course I do," he muttered, forcing a smile. "They are beautiful, Habibti. Like two almonds. Brown almonds, of course. What else..."

He walked around to the side of the bed, changed into his pajamas and slid under the covers.

"Come, let's go to bed. It's been a long evening. Let's get some sleep, so we can start our honeymoon happy and relaxed tomorrow," he said. He patted the covers beside him and gave his wife a mischievous wink.

"Yallah, Habibi, I'm coming," she said, as she reached into her voluminous hair and removed a handful.

"What are you doing, Habibti?" he leapt towards her, his legs tangled in the bed sheets as he collapsed at her feet.

"I was kidding about the sleeping part. You don't have to pull your hair out because of that. I'm sorry! Just stop! Please!" he begged.

"Calm down! I'm just removing my extensions," she said. She held up a bush of curly, blonde hair in front of him. "See? It's fake. It doesn't hurt."

"Of course, it doesn't hurt. It's fake. The hair, the nails…" he snorted, rolling his eyes.

"Come here, Rohi," he beckoned to her. He got up to stand in front of her. He gripped her head at the jawline and pulled it towards him.

"And your hair color? It is not natural either, is it?" he asked, staring at the dark roots sprouting out of the top of her scalp.

"No, I was born with black hair. As black as a crow. But I dyed it blonde for you, Habibi. My mother said you like blondes. Don't you?"

"Yes, yes. Of course. You are just what I asked for in a wife," he muttered, as he crawled back into bed.

"I am so tired. I can't keep my eyes open anymore," he lied and let out a deliberate yawn. "Come, join me in bed and let us start fresh in the morning."

He rolled on his side, his back towards her and closed his eyes.

≈

"It was a beautiful day today, Habibi. Thank you," said Nahla, as she came out of the bathroom in a white hotel robe.

"Yes, it was and you are most welcome," Rami replied. He was sitting on the bed. His reading glasses were perched on the tip of his nose, while he examined a magazine with a serious expression on his face.

"I loved that restaurant by the beach. The fish was so delicious! Although, I felt sorry for that deaf-mute waiter.

He was so friendly but all he could say was 'uh-uh'," she grunted.

"Yes, the poor man. But I actually respect him. He's making the best of his situation," he said, finally looking up from his magazine.

He took off his reading glasses and gave her a worried look.

"You should have put on some sunscreen before leaving the hotel this morning. It looks like you have a sunburn."

"Really?" Nahla gasped. "That's strange. The sun doesn't usually affect me." She turned to the mirror above the dresser to examine her reflection.

"What do you mean? I'm not red anywhere," she said and turned to her husband.

"Your skin is a lot darker than this morning. It looks like you got quite a tan after just one day in the sun. You're lucky it doesn't hurt," he said patronizingly.

"Don't be silly," she giggled. "This is my natural skin color."

"Natural? You're as dark as the Sudanese!" he cried.

"You're exaggerating, Rami! I'm not that black! I just didn't put on my *fond de teint* yet."

"Fondi taaaiin?" he mocked with an angry look on his face.

"Yes, *fond de teint*. It's like a cream you put on your face to lighten your skin tone," she explained, oblivious to his rage.

"I know what fond de teint is. I'm not an idiot," he snapped. "I'm just surprised that you use it. I was under the impression that you, uh – never mind."

"All the women use it," replied Nahla. "I'll go put some on now, if you want."

"No, don't bother. No need to uphold appearances anymore," he sighed. "Just tell me. That nose of yours — the one in the middle of your face. Is it natural or has it been modified in some way or another, as well?"

"My nose?" asked Nahla, shyly. "Why? Don't you like it?"

"Of course, I like it. It's small and cute, like a little cucumber. But I was just wondering if it is the one Allah gave you or is it the work of a surgeon?" Rami persisted.

"Well…to tell you the truth, Habibi, it's not exactly Allah's design. The doctor just straightened it a bit. It was curved like an eagle's beak! I had to get it fixed," she said defensively. "Besides, all the women I know had something done somewhere in their face. Nose jobs, facelifts, you name it. There's nothing wrong with a bit of cosmetic enhancement."

"Yes, I know. They usually go to Beirut, where there are more plastic surgeons than grains of sand on the beach," he muttered and returned to his magazine.

After a long pause, he looked up again and continued. "I'll tell you what, Nahla. Let's cut this vacation short and go visit your mother tomorrow. I'm sure she misses you already."

"My mother? I've only been gone for two days. I'm sure she doesn't mind if we spend the entire week here as planned. Our honeymoon just started, Habibi!" she replied.

"No, I'd rather we head back tomorrow morning. I'm fed up of Kassab," he waved his hand as if to shoo away her protest.

"Besides, I'd like to see some old pictures of you, when you were still a girl in high school. So that I can get to know you better and see what our children might really look like," he snarled. He raised an eyebrow and eyed her suspiciously.

"That is so romantic!" she said fondly, clasping her hands together at her chest. "I was afraid you only loved my looks. I am so relieved, Rami! I can't wait to show you my old pictures and tell you stories about my childhood friends and our adventures," she giggled and snuggled against him on the bed.

"Yes, I can't wait," he mumbled.

❧

"What a nice surprise! What are you doing back already? You're newlyweds. You should be enjoying your honeymoon and not visiting your old mother," said Um Bashar, as she opened the front door.

She gave her son-in-law the mandatory cheek-to-cheek kiss in the air and glared at her daughter over his shoulder.

"Don't worry, Mama," soothed Nahla, beaming at her husband. "Rami wanted to browse through some of my old photo albums to get to know me better."

"Then welcome back! Come in and make yourselves comfortable," said her mother. She ushered the couple into the living room, where Um Nizar rushed to greet them.

"Ahleen[66], Rami, ahleen. A thousand congratulations on your marriage and that gorgeous bride of yours!" she rejoiced.

"This is Um Nizar. She's looking for a wife for her son," explained Um Bashar. "She was so overwhelmed by Nahla's beauty at the wedding that she asked Um Rami to introduce us, so she can get a good look at her sister, Nadine."

"That's wonderful news!" chirped Nahla. "You won't be disappointed! She's beautiful! Not to sound cocky, but we look a lot alike. We're like twins, just two years apart, not two minutes!"

---

[66] Ahleen: welcome.

Um Nizar, visibly irritated by the interjection, turned to Rami. "Who is this woman, Ibni[67]? What is she talking about?" she asked.

"I'm his wife, Nahla, Khaleh[68]," exclaimed the young bride, her eyebrows converging in hurt and confusion. "Don't you recognize me from my wedding?"

Um Nizar stared at her in disgust, and then turned back to the groom. "This is your wife?" she asked, appalled.

"Yes, this is her 'natural look'," Rami answered. "What can I say, Khanum. Things aren't always what they seem."

"Well, then excuse me, Um Bashar. I have to get going," she mumbled, as she rushed out into the hallway.

"Where are you going, Um Nizar? You haven't met my other daughter, Nadine, yet!"

"Never mind, Ikhti. I don't think I'm going to find my son's future bride here. He doesn't like surprises," she muttered, raising a reproachful eyebrow at Nahla.

She nervously fumbled at the doorknob and yanked the front door open. There was a quick "Ma'al salameh[69] " as she slammed it shut behind her.

---

[67] Ibni: term of endearment, literally 'my son'.

[68] Khaleh: term of endearment, literally 'auntie'.

[69] Ma'al salameh: goodbye, farewell, literally 'with safety'.

The house of a tyrant is a ruin.

The Groom's Hand

Salwa fetched the coffee pot out of the cupboard and filled it with two cups of water. She set it on the stove, turned the knob of the smallest burner and pushed it to ignite the hissing gas. The blue flames clambered along the sides of the pot. She added two teaspoons of coffee, a finely ground black powder of Arabica beans and cardamom seeds.

"So, tell me, *Ikhti*[70], how have you been? How are the boys?" she asked her sister, who was sitting at the kitchen table.

"Fine, as always. Firas is working hard and doing well in school. The twins, however, they're driving me crazy. But what am I going to do? Boys their age are just wild," answered Amira, throwing her hands up in the air in resignation.

"And how is that husband of yours? Is he still treating you like a princess?" asked Salwa.

"I can't complain. He's a great help around the house and with the children. Our life is boring but peaceful, *alhamdullilah*," said Amira. "But what about you? How has your husband been treating you?"

"Marwan is great! A wonderful husband!" Salwa quickly replied. Her hand shot up to her eye and brushed a strand of hair onto her face.

"What are you hiding? What happened to your face?" asked Amira. She got up to examine her sister's bruise. "Your eye is black and blue! You look like a raccoon!"

---

[70] Ikhti: literally 'my sister', a term of endearment used colloquially to address friends about the same age.

Salwa grasped the long handle of the coffee pot. She could feel the bubbles clashing against the metal walls, like a volcano about to erupt. She stirred the molehill of coffee powder into the boiling water. A ring of foam began to form and the black froth started to clamber up to the rim of the pot.

"It's nothing, *Ikhti*. It's no big deal," she explained calmly. "I was cleaning the floors yesterday and I slipped and fell on the edge of the coffee table. That's all. It's not as bad as it looks."

"Does your coffee table have four fingers and a thumb?" asked Amira, lifting up Salwa's short *galabieh*[71] sleeve to reveal the red imprints on her upper arm. "I'm your sister! Don't lie to me! Did Marwan do this to you?"

Salwa shrugged and pulled away. She started setting a silver tray with two ornate coffee cups on matching saucers and a glass of water in between.

"Don't make a fuss, Amira," she said. "My husband had his reasons. He had a bad day at work. A man from the health department came by the restaurant yesterday and threatened to shut down the place. It was another one of those corrupt officials, who misuse their position to collect as many bribes as possible before they get caught. Just to be replaced by another thief. Marwan was very upset. Wouldn't you be?"

"Sure, but that's no excuse for him to beat you up. He's a monster and he's using you as a punching bag," retorted Amira, with an accusing frown.

"Don't talk about him like that. *Haram*[72]. Besides, it's not like our father was a holy *Sheikh*, either. He had a short

---

[71] Galabieh: traditional house dress.

[72] Haram: forbidden in Islam.

temper, too. At least my husband atones for his loose hand. Look what he got me when he twisted my wrist."

Salwa spread her arm out in front of her sister and pointed to a thick, golden bracelet.

"He twisted your wrist?" asked Amira, appalled.

"Yes, but it was my fault," she said, waving a dismissive hand at her sister's reproachful look. "I talked back and argued with him. No, wait! That was when he broke my finger. I was so brash. I raised a warning finger to his face. So, he twisted it back until I apologized for being so rude, but it snapped before I could utter a word. But look what he got me for the other finger," she said, her face glowing with joy. She pointed to the golden snake with diamond eyes on her right ring finger.

"It's beautiful, isn't it? And for this black eye, here," she continued, pointing at her face. "He bought me a smart looking dark green pant suit, like the ones the American business women wear on TV. Ah, yes, this golden bracelet – now I remember – I got it when he slapped me so hard, that blood came gushing out of my mouth. But it was nothing serious. Just some torn gums and a wobbly tooth. The dentist fixed it the very next day."

"Are you saying that he gets you an expensive present every time he takes out his anger on you?" asked Amira.

Salwa shrugged again. She turned her attention back to the black brew that was starting to rise. She swayed the pot off the stove and gave it a quick stir. When it began to sink again, she swung it back onto the flames. After three rounds of back and forth, she poured the coffee into two cups.

"Listen, *Ikhti*. Why don't we take the coffee to the bedroom and I'll show you what else Marwan bought me," said Salwa. She balanced the tray in one hand, took her sister's hand in the other and led her down the hall.

"You won't believe the gorgeous outfits he bought me," she continued, as she opened all six doors of her enormous closet.

She showed her sister dozens of silk dresses, fur coats, alligator leather shoes and gold jewelry. She held each piece up against her chest, described the corresponding injury she had incurred and threw it on the bed next to where Amira was sitting.

"The clothes are beautiful. But to tell you the truth, if every one of those cost you a beating, I'm surprised you're still alive!" exclaimed Amira.

Salwa giggled. "You're exaggerating! My husband loves me. He just gets angry sometimes and he has to let off some steam. I'm his wife and there to support him, in the good times and the bad."

Amira shook her head incredulously.

"May *Allah* protect you from your husband's hand," she said pitifully. "*Yallah, Ikhti*. I have to get going. I'm sure my husband is worried already."

Amira stepped into her apartment and was greeted by the moldy odor of cooked nettles. She followed the smell to the kitchen, where her husband was washing the dishes, wearing her red apron. A yellow dish towel slung over his shoulder.

"Welcome home, *Habibti*," chirped Faisal cheerfully when he noticed her in the doorway. "How was your evening with your sister?"

Amira stared at him in silence with a blank expression on her face.

"I made *mloukhieh*[73] and rice. Your favorite," he said nervously, trying to fill the silence. "The laundry is ironed and folded. I helped the boys wash up and tucked them into bed. They finished all their homework, ate their dinner and watched TV for only half an hour. Not a minute more. I promise."

Still no answer from his wife.

"*Habibti*, you look stressed. Why don't you sit down and let me rub your shoulders?" he offered. He pulled out a chair from under the kitchen table and beckoned her to sit down.

"Hit me," mumbled Amira.

"Excuse me?" asked Faisal, confused at his wife's request.

"Hit me," she repeated, her voice now loud and clear. "Slap me! Grab my arm! Just do something!"

"Why would I hit you? I would never raise my hand, not against you or our children," he vowed.

"What kind of man are you? Aren't you frustrated from doing the housework around here? Punch me in the face like a real man or are you a wimp!" she shouted.

"*Habibti*, Amira, calm down," he begged. "Where is this anger coming from? You are my wife. I would never hurt a hair on your head. If it takes violence to prove my manliness, then I'd rather be a wimp!"

Amira slumped into the chair and wrapped her arms around her husband's waist. She buried her face in his stomach.

"Please forgive my outburst. I don't know what I was thinking," she sighed.

---

[73] Mloukhieh: a dish made of cooked nettles and chicken.

If the camel once gets his nose in the tent,
his body will soon follow.

The Greedy Bride

I loved my wife. I still do. She used to be different though. Polite, frugal, modest. She seemed content with what we had and never asked for more. Her transformation was gradual and it all started when she asked me to get her shoe soles fixed.

"Please, don't ever come back with these shoes again! I can't stand the sight of them anymore," the shoemaker pleaded with me.

"What are you talking about? It's your job. You should be happy about the business I'm bringing you," I replied.

"What I mean is that you should get your wife a new pair, my friend. I've fixed those shoes more often than I can count on both hands. Not even a beggar's shoes are this worn out!" he explained. "Please, do us both the favor. Throw them away! For *Allah's* sake!"

"But my wife never asked me for a new pair. She's always been happy with this one. But you're right. I'll go to the Souk this afternoon and surprise her with a brand-new pair of fashionable, high-heeled loafers. *Yallah*, *Hajji*, it's the last time I bring you these shoes," I promised.

That same evening, after dinner, Rana opened the shoebox and unpacked her new black velvet loafers with a golden buckle.

"Thank you, *Habibi*. They are beautiful! But, Fadi, it was really not necessary. I don't need new shoes. The old ones are just fine," she insisted. "You didn't have to waste your money on me like this."

"And what would I spend my money on, if not to make you happy, *Habibti*? What is wrong with a husband wanting to spoil his wife with a small present," I said, pleased with myself.

"Thank you, *Rohi*. May *Allah* bless you and reward you with the thousand-fold, *inshallah*!" she said.

"Why don't you wear them to dinner at my mother's house this evening? You can show them off in front of my sister-in-law," I suggested and bounced my eyebrows provocatively.

"I would love to, Fadi, but I can't," she said.

"Why not?" I asked.

"I can't wear these fancy shoes with my faded skirt and shabby sweater," she pouted.

"Don't you have anything nice to wear?"

She shook her head and stared at her feet in shame.

"Fine, *Habibti*. Don't worry. I'll buy you a new dress at my brother's shop in *Telall*[74] tomorrow," I promised. "You'll look ravishing in it! A beautiful woman like you needs a beautiful outfit!"

The next day, I asked my brother, Shadi, to help me pick out the prettiest evening gown in his store.

"So, you decided to buy your wife a new dress? Did you finally realize that she looked more like your maid than your wife?" he asked. "Did you notice that ugly gray sweater she's always wearing? It looks like it was donated to her by the Red Crescent!"

---

[74] Telall: fashion shopping mile in downtown Aleppo.

"*Yallah*! *Khalas*! Stop criticizing my wife's clothes and help me pick out something nice," I snapped.

We browsed through the winter collection. He pulled out one gown after the other from the racks until we finally agreed on a striped purple pantsuit and a dark red dress with embroidered sleeves.

❧

"They're beautiful, Fadi!" screeched Rana, as she held up her new clothes against her slender body. "I love the colors. The mauve and bordeaux never go out of fashion."

"If you say so, *Habibti*. I don't speak fashion. You, on the other hand, already sound like a chic Madam from Beirut, with your French vocabulary," I said, encouragingly. I was looking forward to seeing her in her new outfit, looking elegant and feminine.

"Come! Let's celebrate with a lavish dinner. A princess like you shouldn't have to cook and do the dishes in her new clothes!" I announced.

She blushed. "You're too kind, *Habibi*! And so generous!" she praised.

"How about the *Jasmin House*? It's in the courtyard of one of the old Arabic houses in *Jdaideh*. I hear they're famous for their delicious grill platters," I suggested. "I'm sure we'll get the best table there, once the waiters see you in your dazzling new dress."

"That sounds wonderful, *Habibi*! But I can't wear this tonight," she sulked and stuffed her new clothes back into the plastic shopping bag.

"But why, Rana?" I pouted. "You have the brand-new shoes I got you yesterday. Don't they match the dress? If you'd rather wear the pantsuit, then go ahead. Just go, put on some make up and change into a new outfit."

"The dress is beautiful and it goes well with the shoes. They're both very suitable for an evening at a fancy restaurant. It's just that…my neck…" she mumbled, rubbing the collar of her scruffy sweater.

"What about your neck, *Habibti*? Does it hurt? Do you have a sore throat?" I asked.

"No, not at all. Don't worry. I'm not sick. It's just that my neck is so bare when I'm wearing this dress," she explained. She lowered her head in shame and stared at her feet.

"Never mind. I'll just wear this gray old thing and we'll get a falafel sandwich in *Mogambo*[75] instead," she continued, tugging at her sleeve. She briefly glanced at me from underneath her furrowed eyebrows, searching for a reaction.

"Fine," I sighed. "I'll buy you a necklace tomorrow. I'll even get you matching earrings, just to get you to change out of that shabby outfit."

"A golden necklace with little diamonds?" she asked, batting her long eyelashes at me.

"With diamonds and rubies if it makes you happy, my queen," I surrendered, without reading much into the devious smile on her lips.

I kept my promise and bought a delicate necklace, lined with small diamonds and a ruby heart pendant, as well as the matching earrings. The jewelry cost me a fortune, but I felt like I owed it to my wife. After all, I thought to myself, she hardly ever asked for anything. Little did I know…

---

[75] Mogambo: district in Aleppo, with fast food restaurants and fashion stores for young people.

"Thank you, Fadi, *Habibi*. They're beautiful," said Rana. She quickly closed the jewelry box, let out an audible sigh and set her gift on the coffee table.

"What's wrong, *Habibti*?" I asked. I could tell that something was bothering her. "Don't you like them? Tell me. I'll return them and get you something else."

"No, they're beautiful. I love them," she said. She got up from the couch and slumped into the armchair across the room, staring at her hands.

"Then tell me, why are you sulking like that?" I demanded.

"It's nothing really. It's just that..." she started and turned to face me, gnawing nervously at her nails. "You know Farida, our neighbor from the third floor? The one with the annoying kids, who are always playing soccer in the entrance of the building."

"Yes. What about her?" I asked.

"Well, her husband gave her a bracelet worth more than 50,000 Liras. A really heavy one, made of white gold with precious stones as big as cherries," she pouted.

"So? The necklace and the earrings that I got you are worth a fortune, too. I paid 8,000 Liras for the set," I retorted.

"And do you know what your sister, Lana, got for her birthday last year?" she continued.

I leaned back in my seat, crossed my arms across my chest and braced myself for a long discussion.

"No. What?" I grunted.

"Her husband got her a brand-new Mercedes," she said eagerly, her eyes popping out of their sockets with envy and rage.

"So? What's your point?" I asked dryly.

"What do you mean, 'So'?" she shouted. "A Mercedes! Do I have to spell it out for you? Your own brother, Shadi, bought a villa for his wife for their tenth anniversary. That's how much he loves her!"

"By *Allah*, you women!" I shouted. "We give you a finger and you take the whole hand!"

Laugh and the world laughs with you;
weep, and you weep alone.

The Bride's Poison

It was eleven o'clock in the morning. Dalal emerged from her bedroom and walked into the kitchen, where she was greeted with a snarky comment from her mother-in-law.

"Good morning, *Mart-Ammi*[76]," said Dalal.

"Finally, the princess woke up and decided to enlighten us with her presence," taunted Nejmieh.

"We stayed up very late last night. Basheer was telling me stories from his work. I couldn't stop laughing until four in the morning. He is so hilarious!" giggled Dalal.

"Stop the silliness and go make us some coffee," barked Nejmieh. "But wash your face first. Did you fall out of bed and into a rainbow this morning? You look like a clown."

"Your son, Basheer, likes my makeup," retorted Dalal, as she put on a pot of coffee. "At least I don't look like a wrinkled old man, *Mart-Ammi*."

"Are you saying I look like an old man, you rude twit! Your husband should slap you around every once in a while. Teach you some manners! That's no way to speak to your mother-in-law," hollered Nejmieh. "You wait and see when he gets back this evening. I'll tell him to knock some sense into your silly little head."

Dalal endured the insults in silence. She served the coffee, head high and chest out, with a resolute expression on her face.

"Here you go, *Mart-Ammi. Tfadali*[77]," she said spitefully and set a cup of coffee in front of her mother-in-law.

---

[76] Mart-Ammi: mother-in-law, literally 'my uncle's wife'.
[77] Tfadali: Please, welcome.

Nejmieh took a sip and cringed. "This brine is disgusting. You are not only a horrible cook, but you can't even make a decent cup of coffee," she complained.

"It's a good thing I had a cup of tea with my son this morning. With breakfast. At eight o'clock. Before he left for work. While you were still sleeping, *Khanum*," she continued and gulped down the rest of the coffee.

Dalal let out an audible sigh. "I don't have to take this from you. Not in my own home," she said. "I'm going out. I can't bear another minute with you in this house."

"Are you going shopping again? Is that all you can do? Spend my son's money and loiter in *Azzizzieh* and *Tellal*? You should stay home and clean this house and cook dinner for your husband!" Nejmieh yelled at her daughter-in-law, who slammed the front door shut behind her.

Dalal came back later that afternoon with her friend, Berlant, and a dozen shopping bags. They had just spread out their new clothes in the living room, when Nejmieh rushed in.

"What's all the commotion?" she shouted. "Why are you two laughing so loud? You sound like loose girls flirting with their Johns!"

She glared at Dalal and raised one eyebrow.

"What are you hiding behind your back?" she asked. "Show me! What are you hiding?"

She lunged at her daughter-in-law and tugged at the skirt in her hand. She freed it from her grip and held it up to examine it.

"Shame on you!" she yelled. "This skirt is far too short! It'll barely cover your knees. *Haram*!"

"But, *Khaleh*[78], it's the latest fashion from Paris," interjected Berlant.

"I don't care if it's from Paris or from Idlib!" said Nejmieh. "You're not wearing that anywhere! You'll ruin this family's reputation, if you dress like a whore!"

"You obviously don't know anything about fashion," retorted Berlant. "You dress like a beggar from *Bab El-Jineyn*[79]."

"How dare you talk to me like that? Who do you think you are?" barked Nejmieh. "Get out of my house! Now! Get out!"

She grabbed the young woman by the arm and dragged her to the front door. Dalal chased after them, trying to hold back her mother-in-law and screaming for her to leave her friend alone.

"And don't you dare come back! You are not welcome in this house!" shouted Nejmieh. She shoved Berlant out into the stairwell and slammed the door shut.

"What did you do?" cried Dalal. "Are you crazy?!"

"She's a bad influence! Rude and cheeky," answered Nejmieh. "We don't entertain silly sluts like her in this house. What would the neighbors say if they saw her in her short skirts and high heels?"

"You had no right to throw her out like that, you shriveled hag!" screamed Dalal. "I won't let you get away with it! You wait and see!"

"I can't stand it anymore, Zuher. She's driving me crazy!" Dalal complained to her brother.

---

[78] Khaleh: term of endearment, literally 'auntie'.

[79] Bab El-Jineyn: neighborhood in Aleppo with a large produce market.

"Hmm," he mumbled.

She roamed the pharmacy while he sorted through supplier invoices behind the counter.

"She's always patronizing me and insulting me," continued Dalal. "I can't live like this anymore, but we can't afford to buy our own apartment yet. So, we're stuck living with that *Ifriteh*[80]!"

She picked up a tube of foot cream from the shelf, cringed and quickly put it back.

"Are you even listening to me?" asked Dalal.

Zuher looked up and sighed.

"Yes, yes. I'm listening. You're miserable because of your mother-in-law," he said. "I've heard it all before. You're like a broken record."

Dalal toyed with a bottle of turquoise mouthwash and strolled between the aisles back to the counter.

"Zuher?" she said.

"Yes, Dalal?" he replied.

"You're a pharmacist. Don't you have anything I can give her that is undetectable?" she asked.

"Undetectable? What do you mean?" he murmured, shuffling the bills around. He licked his thumb and leafed through a pile of papers.

"You know, something I can slip into her drink that can't be detected in an autopsy," she said casually.

"Autopsy? Do you want to kill her now?" he chuckled and pointed at the mouthwash in her hand. "Well, you certainly won't succeed with that."

"I'm serious," she pouted. "It's a daily shouting match with that woman. If I don't get rid of her soon, I'll end up in

---

[80] Ifriteh: monster, dangerous Jinn.

the *Asfurieh*[81]. Basheer will divorce me and I'll have to live with you and your wife."

"No!" he exclaimed, a bit too quickly. "I mean, *Allah* forbid that you should go crazy."

He stroked his thick black beard with a grave look on his face.

"Let me see if I can find a potion for your problem," he said.

He disappeared into the storage room at the back of the pharmacy and reemerged minutes later with a small flask.

"Here you go, *Ikhti*. This should do the job. It's an untraceable poison. Add one drop a day to her coffee or juice and the worms will be gnawing at her in a month," he said.

"A month?" she exclaimed. "Don't you have something more effective? Like rat poison? I saw a woman kill her husband with rat poison on TV. She actually got away with it."

Her eyes lit up in excitement, while her brother's eyebrows knitted in a frown.

"Well, for starters, don't believe everything you see on television. Rat poison can be detected in a blood test. Besides, this is a pharmacy. We don't sell chemicals for pest control," he said.

"This is a powerful chemical. Use only one drop a day. Understood?" he continued. "The police will find traces of it, if you use more. They'll arrest you and hang you in *Bab Al-Faraj*[82]. Believe me!"

"Alright, alright, I got it. I'm not stupid. Give me the bottle already," she said impatiently, snatching it out of his hand.

---

[81] Asfurieh: mental institution, literally meaning 'bird place'.

[82] Bab Al-Faraj: district in old Aleppo, where murderers, rapists and drug dealers are publicly hanged.

"And one more thing, Dalal," he said, holding up a warning finger. "It's very important that you be nice to your mother-in-law to avert any suspicion. Bring her coffee. Compliment her clothes and cooking. Besides, that way she'll be more susceptible to the poisoned beverages you offer her."

"I'll try but it will be very difficult to find something nice to say to that horrid woman," she hissed.

؏

It was almost eight o'clock the next morning. Dalal had set the breakfast table with bread, olives and *labneh*[83].

"Good morning, *Mart-Ammi*," she chirped. "Did you sleep well last night?"

"Good morning," replied Nejmieh hesitantly as she entered the kitchen.

"Basheer will be out in a minute. He is just getting ready for work. Would you like some sugar in your tea?" she asked politely.

Nejmieh, stunned, blinked nervously and shook her head.

"No, thank you," she whispered and pulled out a chair from under the table.

"Then, there you go," said Dalal and placed the small tea glass in front of her. She forced a smile and fluttered her eyelashes, trying to hide an evil smirk.

"I made it especially for you," she whispered.

"Thank you. May *Allah* bless your hands," replied Nejmieh.

"I brought you *barazek*[84] last night. I know it's your favorite pastry," said Dalal. She slid a cardboard box across

---

[83] Labneh: soft cheese made by straining yogurt.
[84] Barazek: sesame cookies.

the table. "We were strolling through the old town when we passed that nice little bakery. You know, the one, where the owner is from Damascus. And I said to Basheer, '*Habibi*, we have to bring some sweets for your sweet mother. She loves *barazek*'. So, we went in and bought you a kilo. Enjoy them, *Mart-Ammi*!"

"Uff! That's really nice of you, but you didn't have to trouble yourself on my account," said Nejmieh, her eyebrows raised in surprise.

"No trouble at all, *Mart-Ammi*. How many mothers-in-law do I have? I deeply cherish you. You are like a crown on my head," she said and knelt down in front of her mother-in-law. "Give me your hand so that I can kiss it."

She gave the back of her hand a peck and pressed it against her forehead. Nejmieh blushed and yanked it back out of Dalal's grip.

"It's alright. Get up. Let's eat breakfast. *Yallah, binti*[85]," she said.

The days passed and accrued to weeks. Dalal carried the small bottle of poison in her bra. She flooded her mother-in-law with extravagant compliments and courteous gestures. She occasionally sought cooking advice from her and cleaned the house without being told. She regularly brought her a glass of orange juice or a cup of coffee, to which she added one drop of poison every day.

Nejmieh, in turn, praised Dalal's manners and admired her taste in fashion.

On the morning of the twenty-third day of her murderous plan, Dalal felt nauseous. She knelt over a bucket on the

---

[85] Binti: term of endearment, literally 'my daughter'.

bathroom floor and started vomiting, while her mother-in-law held her hair back.

"May *Allah* cure you soon, *Habibti*. I can't stand the sight of you suffering," whined Nejmieh. "It must be the salad I made last night. I probably didn't wash it properly. *Allah* send me fever, *inshallah*, for causing you so much pain. I'll never be able to forgive myself."

"Don't talk like that, *Mart-Ammi*. *Allah* forbid anything bad from happening to you," said Dalal. "It's probably just the weather. I feel much better already. I'll just go to my brother's pharmacy this afternoon and get some medicine."

"May *Allah* protect you and bless you with a long life, so you can make my son happy and bear plenty of grandchildren for me," she prayed.

"Zuher, you have to help me," pled Dalal, as she rushed into the pharmacy later that day. "Give me the antidote! I have to save my mother-in-law or she'll die in a week!"

"What are you talking about?" her brother asked.

"The poison! Don't you remember? About three weeks ago, you gave me a flask with poison and told me to put a drop a day in her drink. You said that she'd be dead within a month," explained Dalal.

"So, you don't want to murder your mother-in-law anymore? Why the change of heart?" he asked with a wide grin on his face.

"Ever since I started paying her compliments and pampering her, she's been returning the courtesy. She has become sweet like honey. For example, I've had a stomach flu for the past couple of days. Which reminds me, I need some medicine for that, too, by the way," she said. "Anyway, she held back my hair every morning when I vomited and caressed me like my own mother. I can't bear the thought of hurting her!"

She clasped her hands in front of her and leaned over the counter on her elbows. "Please! Give me the antidote, so I can prevent the worst from happening," she begged.

"Don't worry, *Ikhti*[86]," said Zuher. "There is no antidote and there was no poison. The flask I gave you contained nothing but water."

"Water? Are you sure? *Allah* bless you and thanks to the Almighty! I'm relieved," sighed Dalal. "How did you know I'd change my mind?"

"You're my sister and I know you like the back of my hand. I didn't want you to commit a foolishness that you'll regret your entire life. The solution to your problem was compassion and not murder. You can pull a raging bull by a thread with a kind word. Besides, do you honestly think I would condone a crime like that?"

"No, of course not. But I didn't think I was capable of killing someone either. I was desperate," replied Dalal. "Now that my conscience is clear, my upset stomach might settle."

"It might not have been your conscience that's been causing your nausea, but a little parasite," he said and winked at his sister. "One that will be calling me *Khalo*[87] soon!"

---

[86] Ikhti: literally 'my sister', a term of endearment used colloquially to address a woman of about the same age.

[87] Khalo: maternal uncle.

If you marry a monkey for his money,
the money will go away but the monkey
will stay the same.

The Old Groom

Um Fawzi slapped the copper knocker against the door impatiently. It was only ten o'clock in the morning, yet the scorching August sun was boiling her alive. She loosened the knot under her chin and fanned herself with both hands. Huffing and puffing, she turned around, leaned on the wall and kicked the door with the back of her foot.

"Rashed Beik!" she yelled at the door. "Open the door! It's Um Fawzi!"

When she heard the key turn in the lock, she turned to face the door. She nervously tugged at her coat and adjusted her veil.

An old man opened the door, coughing and clinging to the handle. His cane, with the leaping stallion on its handle, hung from his elbow.

"*Ahlan wa sahlan*[88], Um Fawzi!" he said, snorting between convulsions. "Come in, come in! Why are you still standing at the doorstep?"

The corpulent woman rushed down the hallway and into the living room as he shut the door behind her. He clutched his cane in one hand and pulled up his *galabieh*[89] with the other and wobbled in after her.

The house smelled musty, yet it was cool and moist between its thick walls. A film of dust gathered on the furniture. Old paintings of arid landscapes and a thin curtain of black soot covered the once white walls. The old man's riches were buried under a gloomy veil of neglect.

---

[88] Ahlan wa sahlan: welcome.

[89] Galabieh: traditional Syrian house dress.

"What a pleasure to see you, Um Fawzi," said Rashed Beik indifferently. "Please, sit down and make yourself comfortable."

She unveiled her dyed hair and peeled off her black coat. The small buttons on her dark green blazer, barely clinging to their threads, kept her ample belly covered. Her long skirt, wide at the top and narrow at the ankles, covered her short, stout legs.

"The pleasure is all mine, Rashed Beik," said Um Fawzi with a wide smile on her face.

She fluttered her eyelashes and waved a shy hand at him as she flopped into one of the shabby blue armchairs.

"What can I offer you to drink?" asked Rashed Beik. "A cup of *zhourat*[90] perhaps?"

"Please, don't trouble yourself," said Um Fawzi. She looked around and scowled at the dying plant next to her. "Please. I only came to purchase a wedding gift."

"No trouble at all. The tea is ready and waiting in its pot. I just brewed it ten minutes ago," insisted Rashed Beik.

He poured the hot tea into a small, ornate cup and offered it to his guest. She held it gingerly between two fingers, blew a cloud of steam off the top and slurped loudly.

"May *Allah* bless these hands of yours, Rashed Beik," she praised. "The *zhourat* is delicious."

"Yes, yes. May *Allah* bless you too, *ikhti*[91]," he said. He waved his hand like he was trying to shoo away the compliment.

"You said you needed a wedding gift?" he asked.

---

[90] Zhourat: a herbal tea consisting of a blend of wild flowers, leaves and fruits.

[91] Ikhti: literally 'my sister', a term of endearment used colloquially to address a woman of about the same age.

"Yes, precisely. My neighbor's daughter is getting married next week," explained Um Fawzi. "I was thinking of getting her something fancy of your making."

"Alright then," sighed Rashed Beik. "Let me see what we have here."

He walked over to his work bench in the corner of the room and sifted through a stack of wooden boxes and picture frames. He returned with an adorned, dark brown box. He blew the thick layer of sawdust off the top and coughed loudly as he walked through the dusty cloud.

"How about this inlaid chest? I carved the walnut wood with my own two hands and set every piece of shell in it myself," he boasted.

"A box? No, Rashed Beik, that won't work. I need something bigger and heavier. Something sumptuous. I don't want my neighbors to think I'm stingy," said Um Fawzi.

"But the bride can store her dowry in it," he chuckled to himself and shook his head. "Alright then. I'll look for something bigger and more exquisite," he grumbled and returned to his workbench.

He heaved a small coffee table from behind a large saw and onto his shoulder. He staggered back to his guest, balancing himself on his cane with one hand and the table on his shoulder with the other.

"What are you doing, Rashed Beik? Set it down before you collapse," pled Um Fawzi.

"Don't worry, *ikhti*. I'm ninety-seven years old but I'm still as strong as a horse," he assured her as he coughed.

The brief croak turned into a seizure. His face turned dark red. The coffee table slipped off his shoulder and crashed on the marble floor, chipping off one of its corners. He tumbled down after it and onto his knees, clasping his chest and gasping for air.

Um Fawzi shrieked and ran towards him. She grabbed him under his arms and tried to help him onto his feet.

"Leave me alone! Don't touch me!" he shouted. "I'm alright. I don't need any help."

"May *Allah* help you," she replied. She sighed and gave him a pitiful look.

"Why don't you get an apprentice, Rashed Beik?" she suggested. "You can teach him your handicraft and he'll help you with your work You can even open a shop and let him run it one day while you make yourself comfortable and enjoy a hot cup of *zhourat*."

"I don't trust any aides around here," he said. "They'll exploit me and then they'll go home with their pockets filled like a cow's udder."

"Besides," he continued. "running a shop is too much of a headache — the rent, the taxes and the inventory. I'm happy here. This is my home and my workshop. This is where all the magic happens."

He smiled at Um Fawzi and bounced his eyebrows mischievously. He propped up the small table, examined the damage and leaned on it to get back on his feet.

"But Rashed Beik," she retorted, ignoring his inappropriate flirting. "you're not a young man anymore. You might fall one day and not be able to get back up. There will be no one here to help you. You'll end up like a cockroach on its back, waiting for *Allah*'s mercy."

"*Allah* have mercy on us all," he sighed and sat on the couch across from Um Fawzi. "That's my fate, *ikhti*. I have no one left in this world. No children, nor relatives. If *Allah* wants to take me to His realm when I'm lying helpless on the floor, then so be it."

"Then why don't you get married?" asked Um Fawzi.

"Married? To whom?" exclaimed Rashed Beik.

"There are plenty of women who would jump at the chance to be your wife," she answered. "Don't worry, I'll find you a bride."

"You're tempting me, Um Fawzi," said Rashed Beik eagerly. He giggled into his fist and winked at her. "The thought of marriage makes my heart race and my mouth drool."

"Then there is nothing to stop you," she said excitedly. She glided forward to the edge of her seat with a wide smile and a twinkle in her eyes.

"Hmm…" he said earnestly. "I assure you, *ikhti*, Um Fawzi, I have had a lot of offers in the past," he said. "Reputable families asking for my hand in marriage for their daughters. But I refused every one of them. Do you know why?"

"No. Why?" asked Um Fawzi, surprised at the sudden change in tone.

"Because they were after my money," he replied. "I could see it in their little, beady eyes. Those greedy rats. They wanted to inherit all of this."

He ferociously waved his arms and then started counting on his fingers.

"They want my house, my money, my gold and my treasures. They want the land I own out in Afrin with the olive orchards and the building in *Hamdanieh* that I rented out," he yelled.

"Don't worry, Rashed Beik. I'll find a suitable bride for you. One who is honest and modest. One who wants you for your charming personality and not for your deep pockets," Um Fawzi assured him nervously.

He leaned back in his chair, looked up at the ceiling and scratched his chin.

"Fine then," he said reluctantly. "I've known you for several decades, Um Fawzi. I trust your judgement. Find me a wife. But a young one — no older than twenty years of age."

"Hear, hear! You are ninety-seven years old!" squawked Um Fawzi. "It's like they say, the dreams of cats are full of mice!"

"Age is just a number, *ikhti*," retorted Rashed Beik. "My beard is gray but my soul is blood red. You see, I am young at heart. Some might even call me childish. That's the way *Allah* created me."

"And that is what makes you so charming," said Um Fawzi. She got up and quickly wrapped herself in her coat and veil. She waved at the host and rushed to the door.

"*Yallah*, excuse me, Rashed Beik," she said.

"But Um Fawzi, wait! What about the wedding gift?" he called after her as he teetered down the hallway.

"Forget the wedding gift. I have your wedding to arrange!" she yelled and slammed the front door behind her.

"*Akh, akh*. It's like they say, if someone says there is a wedding ceremony in the clouds, then the women would soon arrive with their ladders," he mumbled. And making his way back to his workbench, he hummed a love song by Um Kalthoum.

Um Fawzi rushed home and frantically called for her niece. She quickly slipped into her *galabieh* and sat cross-legged on the old mattress on the living room floor.

"Mouna, come here, *binti*[92]. I need to discuss an important matter with you," said Um Fawzi out of breath. She beckoned her niece to come closer.

---

[92] Binti: term of endearment, literally 'my daughter'.

The young woman sat down next to her aunt. She propped a pillow against the cold wall and leaned on it.

"What do you think of Rashed Beik?" inquired Um Fawzi. "I mean his morals and his personality. He's pious and polite, don't you think?"

"Well, he's definitely not going to chase after women at his age," Mouna answered. "He's old and weak, like a golden leaf about to fall from the tree."

"Exactly! He's standing with one foot in his grave," said Um Fawzi. "Which is just your good luck!"

"How does that make me lucky?" asked Mouna.

"Because, *Habibti*, he's worth a fortune," explained Um Fawzi.

"I still don't understand," said Mouna. "What does that have to do with me?"

"By *Allah*, do I really have to spell it out for you? If you marry him, you'll inherit all his wealth," said Um Fawzi.

"Marry him!" shouted Mouna. "Are you out of your mind? He's a hundred years old! I'm not going to marry a fossil."

"He's only ninety-seven and he's longing for a young wife to brighten his days," said Um Fawzi. "Besides, he thinks he's still a handsome, young stallion, like the one on his cane."

"Eh, the old monkey looks in the mirror and sees a gazelle," grumbled the young girl.

"Mouna, *binti*, *Habibti*," said Um Fawzi calmly. "Listen to me. You're an orphan. You live here with us under this rented roof. Abu Fawzi and I are old and poor. Our sons live abroad. When we die you will have no one by your side and nothing to call your own. You'll end up on the street like a beggar."

She gently brushed a strain of hair from her niece's face and laid a hand on her arm.

"This marriage will secure your future," she said. "Once Rashed Beik is under the ground, you can marry whomever you want."

"But, *khaleh*[93], he's ancient," pleaded Mouna. "And I am only seventeen. I barely had a chance to live my life."

"You wouldn't have to sacrifice your youth for long. It's just a matter of days or weeks until *Allah* relieves him from his misery. You just have to be patient and *Allah* will reward you with luxury and prosperity."

"I don't know, *khaleh*," sighed Mouna. "If I do marry him, then it would be out of pity and not out of greed."

She pursed her lips to uphold a straight face.

"Are you trying to fool me now?" asked Um Fawzi. "You're not that good an actress. Don't you dare claim the moral high ground. I'm your aunt. I've known you since you were born. I can see right through your lies."

She walked over to her coat hanging on a rusty nail in the hallway. She searched through its pockets and fetched a photograph.

"Here, take this picture. It's from an article about Rashed Beik. Hang it on the wall next to your bed so you can get used to the sight of him."

Mouna gasped as she saw the old man's picture.

"*Allahu akbar*[94]! He's uglier than an ape. He's cross-eyed like a rooster and has more wrinkles than a raisin."

"Stop exaggerating! Remember Mouna, if you don't marry him, someone else might. The women in this town are like vultures circling a rotting carcass," urged Um Fawzi, waving a warning finger. "And if he dies a bachelor, the government will seize all his land and loot his accounts. So,

---

[93] Khaleh: term of endearment, literally 'auntie'.
[94] Allahu akbar: literally "Allah is greater".

hurry up and marry the man, before someone else snatches his fortune."

༺

That same evening, just after the mosque's last call to prayer, Um Fawzi dragged her niece back to Rashed Beik's house.

"*Ahlan wa sahlan*," greeted Rashed Beik as he peered at the women through the spyhole. He yanked the door open and invited them in.

"Come in, come in!" he urged.

"Were you asleep, Rashed Beik?" asked Um Fawzi. "I hope we didn't wake you."

"No, not at all. I'm like a mosquito. I don't sleep and I don't let anyone else get any shut-eye," he chuckled.

Um Fawzi giggled politely, while Mouna ducked behind her, hiding her frown. They followed the old man into the living room and sat on the couch.

"I'm sure you remember my niece," she said pointing at the young woman next to her. "She's very fond of you. She's always raving about you."

"Really?" asked Rashed Beik, eyeing Mouna suspiciously.

"Yes, of course. I'm telling you, just yesterday, she was gushing about how beautiful your handicrafts are. She said she'd love to kiss your talented hands."

Mouna grunted loudly. Her aunt nudged her with a pointed elbow and threw her a threatening glare.

"Yes, she's right, Rashed Beik," Mouna said quickly. "I've always admired your work."

"Thank you, you gorgeous creature," he said. "Did you know that you are absolutely breath-taking? Your eyes are like two olives and your lips are as red as strawberries.

And…uhm…your cheeks are like ripe peaches. If I bite them, they'll drip with juice."

Mouna held the tip of her veil up to her mouth to conceal her disgust.

"Thank you, Rashed Beik," she whispered. "You are so charming."

He winked at her and rolled his eyes from her head, over her plain, pale green dress and down to her worn-out shoes.

"What I also like about you is that you're lean, but not too thin — like a branch, and not too fat like a pregnant cow," he continued. "You're not too tall like a giraffe and not too short, that I'd trip over you."

"It sounds like you like what you are seeing then," proclaimed Um Fawzi.

"Yes, indeed, very much so," said Rashed Beik. "But let me ask you one thing, my little flower, before we get down to business."

"Ask and I will answer, Sir," said Mouna obediently.

"Were you engaged to any other young man before me?" he asked, raising a suspicious eyebrow. His eager eyes bulged out of their sockets.

"Another young man — like you? No, never. I've only had eyes for you," assured Mouna. A mocking smile briefly swept over her lips.

"Yes, there has been a recession in the marriage market these past years. People are demanding exorbitant dowries for their daughters," he stated. "Alas, the girls are turning into spinsters and the men to horny bulls."

He sighed and leaned back in his chair. He fished out a rosary from his pocket and started fumbling with it, in an attempt to appear wiser.

"If they would lower their price, there would be a wedding every night of the week," he continued. "As they say, when the price of wheat goes up, the mules become cheap."

"Who are the mules in this analogy?" asked Mouna indignantly.

Her aunt nudged her and furrowed her brow. "Keep your comments to yourself," she hissed. "And smile, for *Allah*'s sake. You look like you're sucking on a lemon."

She turned to the gray groom and forced a wide smile.

"We won't ask for a single penny from you, Beik," she promised. "My niece just wants to spend the rest of your life – I mean her life, by your side."

"Very well. Then let us discuss the conditions of this marriage," announced the old man.

"*Tfadal*[95]. Let us hear them," said Um Fawzi.

"Look, you angel from the heavens," he said, leaning in closer towards the young woman. "As my wife you will have certain duties."

"Of course, Rashed Beik. I would be disappointed if it wasn't so," said Mouna.

"You'll have to rub my shoulders with ointment in the morning," he said. "And in the evenings, you will undress my feet and bathe them in a tub of hot water and salt."

Mouna nodded. "With pleasure, *khatibi*[96]," she said, yet her wrinkling nose suggested otherwise.

"You'll knead my joints every day, for I have arthritis and my whole body aches at the end of the day," he continued.

"Of course," recited Mouna.

---

[95] Tfadal: an Arabic word used to invite people to share their thoughts, to help themselves to something or to enter a room.

[96] Khatibi: my fiance.

"You will shave the hairs in my ears every week so that I can hear your soft voice whispering words of love and lust," he said.

Mouna frowned, her nostrils flared and her eyes bulged out of their sockets. Her lips slowly parted in an attempt to protest but her aunt quickly intervened.

"That won't be a problem," said Um Fawzi. "It's what a good wife does for her husband. Besides, you are quite a catch, Rashed Beik, with your humor and your good heart. My niece would be lucky to have you."

"I have to be honest with you, though. I do have my faults," he admitted. "I snore like a sawmill, and I have allergies that make me sneeze like a firecracker, just to mention a few."

"No. Really? But you're perfect," exclaimed Mouna, rolling her eyes.

Oblivious to her sarcasm, he lunged forward and fell to his knees at Mouna's feet.

"Oh, I will make you very happy, my white dove," he promised. "I will treat you like a queen on her throne. I will share my bed with you — and my fortune. You are like a crown on my head. I will bathe you in honey and bury you in gold."

He grabbed her hands and pulled them to his mouth for a kiss. She shrieked and jerked back.

"Stop!" she cried. "I mean, it is inappropriate to grope each other before we are officially married before *Allah*."

"Oh, I can't wait to touch your soft skin!" he shouted. "Let us call the *Sheikh* and get married tomorrow. I'm afraid you'll reject me for my old age if we wait too long."

He chuckled to himself and started singing a love song by Sabah Fakhri about two lovers sitting in the garden enjoying the perfume of the jasmine flowers.

❧

The days passed and turned into weeks. Late one morning, about two months after her wedding, Mouna rushed to her aunt's house and frantically banged on the door.

"*Khaleh, Khaleh*," she cried.

"What is it? What happened?" asked Um Fawzi as she opened her front door.

"My husband, Rashed Beik," said the young woman, panting. "He's been asleep for two days straight. He hasn't moved an inch from the couch since Monday."

"Is he dead?" asked Um Fawzi.

"I don't know," replied Mouna. "But he's been a moving corpse for as long as I've known him."

"Come, let's go check then," urged Um Fawzi.

She quickly draped a black veil around her head and the two women rushed down the street to Mouna's new home.

"Let me feel his hands," said Um Fawzi. She kneeled next to the old man and clasped his hand in hers. "They're cold," she said. "Quick! Get me the small mirror from my handbag."

Mouna sifted through the brown purse and passed her aunt a black, round powder box. Um Fawzi opened it and held the mirror under Rashed Beik's nose.

"The mirror is not fogging. He's not breathing," announced Um Fawzi.

"Shall we call the *Hakim*[97]?" asked Mouna.

"You'd better call the *Imam*[98]," replied Um Fawzi. "Your husband is as dead as a dog on the highway. May *Allah* have mercy on his soul."

---

[97] Hakim: literally 'wise man', a common reference to a doctor.

[98] Imam: a Muslim priest.

"Yes! Finally! Thank *Allah* in the heavens!" shouted Mouna, jumping for joy. "I've been waiting for this day for two months now. Rubbing him, washing him and listening to his boring stories, pretending to laugh at his silly jokes."

"Yes, *Allah*, relieved you and he will reward you for your patience," said Um Fawzi. She sprang to her feet and started dancing around her niece, yodeling gleefully. "Congratulations! You are now a wealthy widow!"

"You wretched hags!" yelled Rashed Agha. The two startled women screeched as the old man got up from the couch. His face red with rage and his gray hair disheveled.

"By *Allah*, he's alive!" cried Um Fawzi.

"I'm alive and kicking, you greedy whores! And I heard everything you said! You were after my money, just like everyone else," he roared and pointed at Mouna with a threatening finger. "As for you, you two-faced witch! I hereby divorce you! I divorce you! I divorce you! There, I said it three times, which makes it legally binding!"

Mouna gasped at the phrase every Syrian woman dreaded. She saw her life crumble before her eyes. As a penniless divorcée, her chances of finding a new husband were next to nothing. She fell to her knees, clasped her face in her hands and sobbed.

"Calm down, Rashed Beik," pleaded Um Fawzi. "There is no need to rush into any important decisions."

"Get out! Get out of my house! The both of you!" he yelled. "I'm fed up with all of you — gold diggers! I will donate all my earthly belongings to charity!"

He grabbed each of the women by the arm and dragged them out the door. He pushed them onto the street, trotted back into his house and slammed the door shut behind him.

Lying is a disease, and truth is a cure.

The Bride's Gown

Iman was lying on her bed, twirling her short brown hair around her finger. She stared at the ceiling with a sheepish smile on her lips.

"He's so handsome," she said to her friend Sahar across the room, who was sitting on the desk dangling her long legs and examining her fingernails.

"Who?" asked Sahar absent-mindedly. She gnawed on a piece of loose dry skin at the tip of her middle finger.

"Who do you think?" snapped Iman. "My fiancé, Ziad, of course."

"Ah, yes," said Sahar. She jumped off the desk and onto the floor by the bed. She crossed her legs and tilted her head attentively to listen to her friend ramble about her future husband.

"Did I tell you, he's a doctor in Canada?" continued Iman.

"Yes, on several occasions," answered Sahar. "But I'm worried you never met him in person. Do you at least talk on the phone every once in a while?"

"Not as often as I'd like," sighed Iman. "He's very busy, you know. He's a famous surgeon there. If he's not in surgery, then he's visiting his patients or lecturing medical residents about new techniques and equipment."

"So, you barely know him," said Sahar.

"I know enough to be confident that I want to spend the rest of my life as Mrs. Ziad Salateh," insisted Iman. "Besides, he's moving back to Aleppo in two weeks, so we'll have enough time to get acquainted before the wedding."

"*Inshallah*[99]," said Sahar.

"The Martini Hospital wants him as the new head surgeon there," bragged Iman. "He's going to buy us a villa in *Shahba*, and he promised me a white Mercedes."

"Only one? *Eh*, you deserve a whole flock of Mercedes and Jaguars! Quick, crack your knuckles to pop the eyes of the envious!" urged Sahar and giggled.

"You're so superstitious," said Iman smiling, yet she obeyed her friend.

Sahar freed her long, black mane from its clip and brushed it onto one shoulder. She ran her fingers through it and divided the waterfall into three thick strands.

"But he's divorced, right?" she asked, while her nimble fingers braided her hair.

"Yes, but his first wife was a *Ifriteh*[100]," said Iman.

"That's what all men say about their ex-wives," said Sahar.

"But it's true! Ziad's mother told me," insisted Iman. "She said she had no sense of humor whatsoever. She took everything literally and felt insulted by every comment. It was like poking a hornet's nest."

"Uff," said Sahar.

"And she was very thin — only skin and bones," continued Iman. "The most talented butcher wouldn't be able to cut a kilo of meat off her ribs."

"But some men like lean women," pouted Sahar and looked down at her flat chest and bony legs.

"And she was stupid too," said Iman, ignoring her friend's discomfort. "Her brains were like two nuts in a cup — rattling. She barely finished fifth grade. That's what Um Ziad said."

---

[99] Inshallah: literally 'if Allah wishes'.
[100] Ifriteh: monster, dangerous Jinn.

She sat up and swung her legs over the edge of the bed. She leaned towards her friend with a fierce look on her face.

"And her family was rude. Not once did they invite the groom's family to dinner!" said Iman. She raised her hands in fury. "They're arrogant too, and they don't fear *Allah*. They'd kill a man and attend his funeral."

"Then it's a good thing your Ziad divorced her," said Sahar.

"Yes, he divorced her after only three months," said Iman. "He gave her the *muakhar*[101] with a cherry on top and sent her back to her parents' house."

"Let's change the topic, *ikhti*. Talking about marital problems is ruining my good mood," Sahar urged. "Did you order a dress from the seamstress yet?"

Iman sighed and reached for the bridal magazine on her night table.

"No, not yet," she said and flipped through its pages.

Sahar swung her thick braid onto her back, got up from the floor and crawled onto the bed next to Iman. She gently rubbed her friend's neck and rested her chin on her shoulder.

"What about that dress?" asked Sahar, pointing at a picture in the magazine on Iman's lap. "You'll look dazzling in it."

"No way, are you crazy?" exclaimed Iman. "I can't wear that! It's sleeveless! My father will kill me for exposing my naked shoulders like that."

"OK, then what about that cream one there?" asked Sahar and pegged another glossy bride.

"It's nice," sighed Iman. "But it won't look as good as it does on this model if I get it made here. Um Ahmad is good,

---

[101] Muakhar: The dowry, mahr, can be paid partially: the mukadam up front when signing the marriage contract and the muakhar when death or divorce separates the couple.

but she's an amateur compared to the professionals in Europe and Turkey."

"Iman, *Habibti*, she's the best we've got and even she will have to work on your dress day and night from now up until the big day to finish it on time," urged Sahar. "You have to find a dress soon. Your wedding is in two months."

"I know, I know," said Iman.

"Or you could just buy one from the *Souk*," suggested Sahar.

"No! I'd rather wear a potato sack to my wedding than a dress from the *Souk*," Iman insisted. "Um Ahmad is the only seamstress I trust in this country. The dresses from the *Souk* are rags, decorated with tacky sequin flowers and barely held together by a few sloppy stiches. I tried one on the other day. I'm telling you, Sahar! The sleeves weren't even the same length and the neckline was crooked."

She flipped the page angrily, took a deep breath to calm herself down and gazed out the window.

"I didn't mean to upset you. You're absolutely right about the *Souk*," agreed Sahar. "But where are you...?"

She snatched the magazine out of her friend's hand and held it up to her nose.

"Look," she nudged Iman and pointed to an ad in the classified section. "Someone is selling their wedding dress!"

"You want me to wear a second-hand dress to my wedding?" exclaimed Iman.

"Wait! Listen to me," said Sahar and read the ad out loud. "It says here, 'Wedding gown. Imported from Paris. Color egg shell. Size 38. Fair price. Call 021-2266711.' It was made in France. What more do you want?"

"It's used," said Iman. "Some other girl wore it to her wedding."

"You can get it cleaned! She probably only wore it once. I'm sure it's still intact and as good as new," said Sahar.

"Why don't we go and take a look? What do you have to lose? You can always go back to sifting through the magazines if you don't like it."

"Alright," Iman agreed. "I'll call her and make an appointment to see the dress."

She kept her promise and arranged to pass by the following evening.

❧

"Welcome, girls, please, make yourself comfortable," Um Tawfik ushered Iman and Sahar down the hallway and waved at the green armchairs in the middle of the living room.

"What can I offer you to drink? A coffee maybe? Or a glass of orange juice?" she asked.

"Please, don't trouble yourself, *Khaleh*[102]," said Sahar. "We're only here to see the wedding gown."

"No trouble at all," said Um Tawfik.

A slender, young woman appeared in the doorway. She had olive green eyes, peach pink skin and cherry red lips. Her curly brown hair was tied in a loose bun at the back of her head.

"*Marhaba*[103]," she said. "*Ahlan wa sahlan*[104]."

"This is my daughter, Nisrin," said Um Tawfik and turned to her. "*Binti*[105], please get these beautiful ladies some orange juice, *Habibti*."

"*Hader*[106], Mama," the young woman replied. She hurried into the kitchen and promptly returned with a tray

---

[102] Khaleh: term of endearment, literally 'auntie'.

[103] Marhaba: hello.

[104] Ahlan wa sahlan: welcome.

[105] Binti: my daughter.

and four glasses of orange juice. She offered each of the women a glass and sat down next to her mother on the couch.

"If I may ask," said Iman shyly. "I mean – I assume it is your dress that you're selling, isn't it?"

"Yes, it's mine," answered Nisrin. A sullen look crept over her face. She pursed her lips until they turned pale.

"Excuse my asking," said Iman. "but why would you want to sell your wedding dress? It bears a dear memory of the most special day of your life."

"Most women treasure their wedding dresses, but I can't wait to get rid of mine. It just reminds me of the biggest mistake of my life," explained Nisrin.

She laid her hands on her knees and stared at them. "You see, I'm in the middle of a divorce," she whispered.

"Oh, we're sorry to hear that," said Sahar. "May *Allah* assist you in these difficult times and send you a groom better than the first."

"Any donkey would be better than that wretched husband of yours," cursed Um Tawfik. Sahar jumped in her seat, startled by the host's outburst.

"That bad?" asked Iman.

"He's a drunk gambler with a temper! Pretending to be a big shot surgeon. He doesn't even have a medical degree yet," complained Um Tawfik.

"*Haram*[107]!" exclaimed Iman.

"If it wasn't for her uncle in Toronto, who helped my daughter escape on a moonless night last month, she would still be stuck in Canada with that monster," cried Um Tawfik.

---

[106] Hader: term of obedience, literally 'ready'.

[107] Haram: forbidden in Islam.

"Calm down, Mama," pled Nisrin. She dug her fingernails into her mother's arm and flashed her a desperate glare. "I'm sure our guests don't want to hear you rant about my ex-husband."

"No, we don't mind at all," interjected Iman, hungry for more gossip.

"He doesn't even have a place to live over there," continued Um Tawfik. "They squatted in the hospital dorms, using the public restrooms and eating bread and salt in the cafeteria."

"Excuse me for being blunt, but why didn't you ask around before agreeing to give him your daughter?" asked Sahar.

"We asked about him all over town," assured her Um Tawfik. "His reputation was impeccable. We fell for his looks, his charms and his flashy car."

She sighed and shook her head. She turned to her daughter and held her hand.

"And the bastard is holding her hostage now," she said.

"How's that?" asked Sahar.

"He won't agree to the divorce," answered Um Tawfik. "He wants the dowry and the jewelry back as well as the money he spent on the wedding and the engagement parties. It all adds up to more than 250,000 Liras. He calls us ten times a day, threatening us, and asking whether we were able to raise the money yet."

"We hope to add whatever amount we get for the wedding gown to the pot," whispered Nisrin. "I just want to pay him off so that he'll leave me alone."

"*Allah* punish you, Ziad, for your sins in the burning flames of *Jihanam*, you no good son of whore!"

"His name is Ziad?" asked Sahar. She looked over to Iman, who had suddenly turned pale.

"Yes," affirmed Um Tawfik.

"And he's a doctor in Canada?" asked Iman in a feeble voice.

"Yes, why? Are you alright, *binti*? You look sick," asked Um Tawfik.

"What is his family name?" asked Sahar.

"Salateh. His name is Ziad Salateh. Son of Mazen Salateh from the *Mogambo*," said Um Tawfik.

Iman's hand slid off her lap and her glass fell to the ground. She slouched in her seat and covered her face with both hands.

"She's his new fiancée," explained Sahar. "They're getting married in two months."

"Not anymore, we're not!" said Iman, her voice loud and determined. Her sorrow had quickly turned into anger. "I'll show that cheating liar that he can't do this to us."

"What are you going to do?" asked Sahar.

"You'll see," smirked Iman. She bit her lower lip and her eyes twinkled with revenge.

❦

Two weeks later, Ziad returned to Aleppo, bearing gifts for his beautiful bride. Iman had made sure to order exquisite handbags, designer jewelry and fancy clothes from her soon-to-be husband.

The young couple reunited that same evening at the *Jasmin* restaurant in an old Arabic house in *Jdaideh*. They sat at a table next to the fountain in the courtyard. The sound of the *Oud*[108] filled the hot summer air.

---

[108] Oud: a pear-shaped instrument, similar to a guitar, commonly used in Middle Eastern music.

"Just so you know, *Habibti*, you cost me a fortune," he said and leaned over the table to kiss Iman's hand. "But you are worth every penny, my queen."

"Thank you, *Habibi*," she replied and waved at the bags next to his chair. "Let me see them, Ziad. Hand them over."

"You are very impatient, *Rohi*[109]," he said and set them on the table in front of her. "I hope you like them."

She took a quick peek into each of the bags to make sure everything was there and turned back to her fiancé.

"Thank you so much, Ziad," she said, smiling. "I will never forget how good you were to me. I have a present for you, too."

"Really?" asked Ziad eagerly and winked at her. "I hope it's something nice for our wedding night."

She glanced at the restrooms, nodded and smiled. He followed her gaze and looked over his shoulder. He suddenly turned pale at the sight of the ghost from his past.

"What in *Allah*'s name?!" he yelled. "What is *she* doing here?"

"Nisrin is here to pick me up. We're going out for coffee," said Iman. "Thanks again for the presents. I'll make sure she gets back what you stole from her."

She walked towards her new friend, loaded with her presents, giggling.

"By the way, the wedding is off!" she called over her shoulder.

The girls strolled out of the restaurant arm-in-arm leaving behind a shell-shocked fiancé and ex-husband.

---

[109] Rohi: term of endearment, literally meaning 'my soul'.

151

Everyone is critical of the flaws of others,
but blind to their own.

Imperfect Groom

Houda peered over her cup as she took a sip of coffee. Her date didn't seem too bad. He was ruggedly handsome. His pale skin was as white as the inside of a coconut. He needed a new set of teeth and he was too thin for her liking but she couldn't afford to be a choosy beggar.

She was thirty-five years old, average looking with wavy, short brown hair and brown eyes. She lived with her brother and his wife. She felt like a leech, and longed to escape from their reproachful looks and snarky comments. Her husband had divorced her after seven childless years, just to replace her with his fertile secretary.

Alas, she thought to herself, it was time to move on and find someone new. The matchmakers called her a hopeless case. Her sister-in-law considered her worthless. With no one to broker her next marriage, she decided to turn to the dating section in the local newspaper.

That is where she found Talal. He had suggested skipping to the chase and meeting up the next day rather than delaying their encounter with embellishing phone calls.

"I'm very glad you were free this evening," he said, interrupting her daydream.

"Yes, actually I'm free every evening," she quickly replied. Her face froze in shock when she suddenly realized that she had just admitted to being a spinster.

"I mean, uhm – I'm usually not free in the evenings. Luckily, my friend had to cancel today, because her son is sick," she lied nervously. "I mean, why don't you tell me about yourself?"

She sighed and covered her mouth with both hands as if to prevent more embarrassing words from escaping.

"Well, I'm forty-two years old. My star sign is Taurus," he said, chewing vigorously. The pink gum in his mouth bounced off his teeth and jumped from the inside of one cheek to the other.

"Excuse me, *Ustaz*[110] Talal," Houda interrupted. "Would you mind, if it's not too much to ask…would you please remove that chewing gum from your mouth. It would help me concentrate on what you're saying."

"I'm sorry, *Anseh*[111], but I can't," he replied.

"Excuse me?" asked Houda, raising an incredulous eyebrow.

"This is a non-smoking restaurant," he explained. "I need the chewing gum to calm my nerves until I can go out later to smoke a cigarette."

"You're a smoker?" exclaimed Houda. "But it's bad for your health. You might get cancer because of it one day."

"I know, I know," he said, seeming annoyed about being lectured. "I tried switching to the *argileh*, but I just don't like the taste. It just doesn't accentuate the flavor of the *Arak*[112] as much as the cigarette."

"*Arak*?" she asked, astonished. "So, you drink?"

"Yes, I drink. I'm not particularly religious. I believe in *Allah*. And what is in the heart is what really matters — not the fasting and the praying like a hypocrite," he said. "Is that a deal-breaker for you?"

---

[110] Ustaz: a polite form of addressing a man. Literally meaning Mister or teacher.

[111] Anseh: a polite form of addressing a woman. Literally meaning Madam or teacher.

[112] Arak: a distilled, anise-flavored alchoholic drink about 40-60% proof.

"No, no," whispered Houda. "You're not hurting anyone, so..." Her voice trailed off as she tried to fight her disappointment.

"Don't worry, *Anseh* Houda," he assured her. "I only drink when I'm in the casino. Never at home."

"The casino?" she exclaimed. "So, you gamble, too?" Her eyebrows crept over her forehead in surprise. Her nostrils flared briefly. Her jaw dropped slightly. She set her elbows on the table and held her head in her hands and braced herself for more letdowns.

"Yes, the owner of the casino down in *Azzizieh* is a friend of mine from prison. He always lets me in on some back-alley poker games with some big whales. And by *Allah*, I always win. Just last night, I made fifty thousand in one game!" he said, chuckling to himself.

Houda's eyebrows flew up to her hairline. Her eyes almost burst out of their sockets.

"You were in prison?" she shouted.

"Yes, I'm not proud of it, but we all make mistakes," he said. "They released me just last month after nineteen years for good behavior. I'm a changed man now. I assure you."

She suddenly saw the signs: the pale skin from being incarcerated in a dark cell for almost two decades; the rotten teeth and the lean figure for the lack of a tooth brush and sufficient food.

That was one fault too many. She didn't want to spend the rest of her life alone, but she wasn't desperate enough to marry an ex-convict. She snatched her phone from the table and threw it in her purse. She grabbed her coat from the back of her chair and got up to leave.

"Excuse me, *Ustaz* Talal," she said. She took a step away from the table and opened her mouth again to deliver a lame excuse but her curiosity subdued her.

"Why were you sentenced to almost two decades in prison? What did you do?" she asked.

"I killed a young woman," he admitted. "I met her during my studies at the Aleppo University. She refused to go out on a second date with me. She ignored me entirely after just one short rendezvous in the campus cafeteria."

"So, you killed her?" asked Houda. She tightly clutched her coat and slowly slid back into her seat.

"It was out of anger. It suddenly came over me one day. I went to her parents' house and I beat her to death with my bare hands. Right there, in the doorway. She wouldn't let me in that bitch," he replied. He slammed his fist on the table.

"Argh!" he growled. He took a deep breath, stroked his chest with his palms and exhaled slowly and loudly.

"But don't worry, *Anseh* Houda! Prison taught me patience. By *Allah*, when you spend nineteen years trapped in a cage like an animal, you have no choice but to be patient."

Houda stared at him. Her eyes were wide open in shock yet her lips were stretched into a forced smile. Her foot nervously tapped the floor under the table.

"Of course, *Ustaz* Talal," she said anxiously. "What an interesting man you are. I would love to see you again soon."

All too often people concentrate on finding
the right spouse, little realizing that half of any
marriage is being the right spouse.

– Yasir Qadhi

The Bride's Cake

A woman, wrapped in a black robe, rushed into the notary's office. She unraveled her face from under her niqab and awkwardly fell to her knees in front of his desk with a loud thud.

"*Kateb Al-Adel*[113], you have to help me. May *Allah* bless you! I want to divorce my husband," she pleaded. Her face cringed in pain.

"Divorce. I see," said the notary. "*Bismillah, Alrahman, Alraheem*[114]."

He scratched his thick, gray beard and adjusted the small reading glasses perched on the tip of his nose and peered at his visitor from over them, wrinkling his forehead.

"Your kind name, please," he said. He licked the tip of his thumb and started browsing through a thick log lying on the desk in front of him.

"Samakieh. Nawal Samakieh, daughter of Fateh Samakieh. My husband's name is Bilal Tarabishi, Your Honor," she panted. She leaned on the seat of the wooden chair next to her with one hand and pushed herself off her knee with the other, as she heaved her ample curves onto her sturdy legs.

"And how long have you been married?" he asked.

"Almost six months," she answered.

"So, you are newlyweds. Congratulations," he said earnestly.

---

[113] Kateb Al-Adel: notary.

[114] Bismillah, Alrahman, Alraheem: In the name of God, most gracious, most compassionate.

"There's nothing to congratulate me for," she pouted. "I can't stand being married to Bilal anymore."

"And why is that? Is he violent? Did he mistreat you?"

She clicked her tongue in denial. "No, he never raised his hand in anger."

"Did he betray you with another woman and disgrace you?"

She shook her head.

"Did he deny you your dowry?"

"No, nothing like that," she said. She waved her hands in front of her, shooing away the notary's presumptions.

"Then why do you want to divorce him?" he asked.

"He's been neglecting me ever since we got back from our honeymoon. His nose is always buried in some history book or he's busy browsing a scientific journal. All he talks about is politics, science and technology. I don't care if elephants are pregnant for almost two years or if some German astronaut went to a space station somewhere in the galaxy," she complained. "And to make things worse, he makes fun of me when I let him in on the latest gossip about our neighbors and relatives. He makes me feel silly and stupid. I can't stand being married to him anymore."

"Hmm, I see," sighed the notary. "There is no hope for your marriage, then?"

"No hope at all, *Kateb Al-Adel*," replied Nawal. "For *Allah's* sake! I'm begging you. Grant me a divorce and relieve me from my agony."

"Fine, woman, fine. I'll look into your case. Come back in a week and I'll see what I can do for you," he said.

"Thank you, Your Honor. Thank you! May *Allah* bless you! You are indeed fair and wise!" she said. She bowed lightly in gratitude, hurriedly covered her face with her black veil and turned to leave the notary's office.

"Just one thing before you go," he called after her as she reached the door.

She turned around to face him. "Anything, Your Honor," she whispered from behind her veil.

"Bring me a cake next time," he demanded.

"A cake?" she asked.

"Yes, a cake. Bake it yourself and borrow all the ingredients from your neighbors," he said. "Understood?"

"But why should I go around begging my neighbors for flour and baking powder? I have everything I need at home. They'll think I'm poor and that my husband is broke," she said.

"Don't question my reasons, just accept my judgement," he ordered.

"As you like, *Kateb Al-Adel*. I will do as you ask. Your wish is my command," said Nawal.

❧

The next day, Nawal set out to gather the ingredients for the notary's cake. She decided to borrow flour from her neighbor, Um Jihad, from the first floor.

"*Al-salamu alaikum, jarti*[115]," greeted Nawal when her neighbor opened the door.

"*Wa alaikum al-salam*," answered Um Jihad. "*Marhaba.* Welcome, welcome. *Tfadali*[116]. Come in."

"I won't keep you for long, *jarti*. I just wanted to borrow some flour from you, if you don't mind," said Nawal.

"Flour? Of course! You can have all the flour you want. But come in and have a cup of coffee with me. It's not nice to chat on the doorsill like this," urged Um Jihad.

---

[115] Jarti: my neighbor.
[116] Tfadali: please, welcome.

"*Yallah*, if you insist," Nawal quickly gave in and followed her inside. "But I really can't stay long."

"What do you need the flour for? Are you baking a cake?" asked Um Jihad. She guided her guest into the kitchen.

"Yes, a cake for *Kateb Al-Adel*. He asked for one in return for facilitating my divorce," replied Nawal. She peeled off her scarf and made herself comfortable on one of the wooden chairs at the table.

"Divorce? Why in *Allah*'s name would you want a divorce?" exclaimed Um Jihad. Her hands started making the coffee, while her ears attentively listened to Nawal.

"What can I tell you, *jarti*. Life with my husband has become unbearable. He ignores me most of the time. And when he does look up from one of his thick books, he makes fun of me for taking interest in other people's lives. He says my friends and I are like a bunch of clucking hens with nothing better to do than to talk about one another behind our backs," she pouted. "So, tell me, Um Jihad, don't I have the right to ask for a divorce, when he's making me feel so miserable?"

"I'm surprised! You seemed like such a happy couple. Please, reconsider. You shouldn't rush such an important decision like this," pleaded Um Jihad. She served the coffee and sat across from her neighbor at the table.

"I've already made up my mind. I cannot stand another one of his crude comments!" insisted Nawal.

"By *Allah*! Unbelievable! He seems like such a nice man! Not like my husband, the drunk," moaned Um Jihad.

"Your husband drinks?" gasped Nawal. "But it's *Haram*[117]!"

---

[117] Haram: forbidden in Islam.

"He doesn't only drink. He's always drunk!" complained Um Jihad. "He comes home every evening, with a frown on his face and bottles clattering in a black plastic bag in his hand. His mood worsens with every sip, until he vents his anger on my face. After beating me senseless, he collapses on the couch and vomits himself to sleep."

"What a *kafir*[118]! May *Allah* protect you from him, *jarti*! Is that how you got that black eye?" said Nawal.

"I got this after a vodka binge," explained Um Jihad, pointing to her tired face. "Believe me, *Ikhti*[119], he taught me the names of all the liquor brands that money can buy. Arak, whiskey, gin," she said, counting on her fingers. "And I can tell from the type of drink how long it will take before he lapses into a coma. Our home smells like a dirty bar and my children are scared of their father. They hide in their rooms as soon as they hear his key turn in the lock."

She sighed loudly, took a sip of her coffee and stood up.

"I've complained enough already. I don't want to trouble you with my problems. By *Allah*, you apparently have plenty of your own! Let me fetch the flour for you, so that you can get your divorce," she said.

Um Fawzi, on the second floor, peered out from behind her front door. A strand of her thick gray hair fell out from under her black scarf.

"*Ahlan*[120], *jarti*!" she said, opening the door a little further.

---

[118] Kafir: a sinner or unbeliever.

[119] Ikhti: literally 'my sister', a term of endearment used colloquially to address friends about the same age.

[120] Ahlan: welcome.

"Excuse me, Um Fawzi," said Nawal. "I just wanted to ask you if I could borrow some sugar, please."

"Of course. Come in, come in," said the elderly woman, her wrinkled face crumpled into a smile. "What do you need the sugar for?"

They made themselves comfortable in the dining room. Nawal told her neighbor about the meeting with the notary, his unusual request and her marital problems.

"To cut a long story short, you're bored! That's why you want to divorce your husband? Out of boredom?" asked Um Fawzi, raising a skeptical eyebrow. "Go back to him and kiss his feet, you silly woman! Be grateful that he isn't like mine," she reprimanded.

"Why? What is wrong with your husband, *Khaleh*[121]?" asked Nawal.

"Do you see my gray hair? I am forty-three years old but I look like an old hag," complained Um Fawzi. "It's because I worry. I worry every day about how I'm going to feed my children. How I'm going to afford to buy their school uniforms and textbooks!"

"Why, Um Fawzi? Tell me! Did your husband lose his job at the fabric factory?" asked Nawal.

"No, *jarti*. He still has his job, but not a single penny reaches this house. You see, my husband is a gambler," explained Um Fawzi. "He stops at the horse tracks or at his friend's house for a game of cards after work, where he spends his entire day's earnings. He already wasted my dowry and my jewelry on his hopeless bets."

"Does he ever win anything?" asked Nawal.

"Never. Not once," answered Um Fawzi. "*Allah* banned gambling for just this reason. It's the Devil's hobby. I'm

---

[121] Khaleh: term of endearment, literally 'auntie'.

stuck here feeding my children plain bulgur with fried onions every evening and mending their ragged clothes."

"May *Allah* support you in these difficult times, *inshallah*!" said Nawal, raising her hands in prayer.

"So, I'm begging you, *jarti*," sobbed Um Fawzi. "Think twice before you decide to divorce your husband. Talk to him. Try to hash things out and be grateful that *Allah* sent you a decent man, who cares for you — a man whose biggest fault is his intellect."

She got up, headed towards the pantry and returned with a dark plastic bag. "Here's the sugar you wanted," she said. "*Inshallah*, it will sweeten your marriage and not ruin it."

❧

"Cake?! *You*? You want to bake a cake?" asked Lama incredulously, her eyes gleaming with curiosity. "You're hiding something from me, Nawal. I can smell a secret from a mile away. Tell me! What's really going on?"

"It's not a secret, really. I want to divorce my husband. I'm fed up with his know-it-all attitude and his hurtful remarks. I consulted the notary and he asked for a homemade cake as a remuneration," explained Nawal, following her neighbor into the living room.

"I knew it! I knew there was something wrong," said Lama. She leaned back in her armchair. Her dark red hair appeared purple under the faint light of the chandelier dangling from the ceiling. "Nonetheless, I think you're making a big mistake. He's a good man, your Bilal. At least his eyes don't wander."

"Why would they wander?" asked Nawal, obviously insulted.

"Some men can't control themselves. Take my husband, Fares. He hasn't seen a skirt he hadn't chased after yet. He's like a bumble bee, jumping from one flower to next," Lama pouted.

"Really! You poor thing, *Habibti*," said Nawal compassionately. "May *Allah* stick needles in his eyes, that *Ibn Al-Haram*[122]!"

"The other day, he came back home late at night. He claimed he was at a business dinner. That filthy liar! That man can't utter a word of truth, even if he swallowed the entire Koran," announced Lama.

"What made you think he was lying?" asked Nawal.

"I could smell the stench of women's perfume on him when he walked through the front door. Like he had wallowed in a bed of roses. Then I found a long blonde hair on his jacket," said Lama, her eyes fierce with anger.

"I'm so sorry for you, *jarti*," said Nawal. "But at least he still comes home to you."

"He comes home, yes, but not to me. I could dance half-naked in front of him, like in those Indian movies, and he wouldn't look up from his phone," Lama complained. "And when I wear makeup and try to seduce him with smoky eyes and deep red lips, he makes fun of me. He says I'm too old to flirt like Brigitte Bardot."

She wiped a lonely teardrop from her cheek.

"What a rude brat your husband is! Don't worry, Lama! You are as beautiful as you were ten years ago. He's blind not to see it!" said Nawal, laying a soothing hand on her friend's shoulder.

"I wish I was ten years younger. I should have divorced that man while I still had the chance. Back then, *Ikhti*, I could have replaced him within two days. The admirers were queuing around the block. *Yallah*, it is my fate. It's what *Allah* has written for me," sighed Lama. She heaved herself

---

[122] Ibn Al-Haram: bastard, literally meaning 'son of sin'.

out of her armchair and walked towards the door. "Let me get you those eggs and the baking powder that you wanted."

≈

"Here is your cake, Your Honor," said Nawal.

"Thank you, *Khanum*, but to what do I owe this gift?" asked the notary.

"But, *Kateb Al-Adel*, you asked me to bake you a cake in return for granting me a divorce from my husband," explained Nawal. "Forget I ever asked, though. I decided to accept his faults. *Allah* forbid I ever leave his side. He's a real blessing compared to other men."

About the author

Anna Halabi was born and raised in Aleppo, Syria. She immigrated to Europe in 1999 to pursue her university studies. She currently lives with her family in Germany.

The stories and characters in this collection are inspired by her personal experiences, as well as those of her relatives and friends.